"You!" Kerri hi... her tracks, her feet planted firmly in Nina and Elizabeth's path. "I knew you were after me! How long have you been following me?"

Nina put her hands up, palms out as if to deflect Kerri's fury. "Nobody's following you, Kerri. We were just on our way back from —"

"Shut up!" Kerri screeched. Her shrill voice echoed across the campus. In the distance, Nina saw a few heads turn with surprise in their direction. "I know you're lying! You want to kill me *dead* . . . well, it's not going to happen!"

All at once Nina felt as if she were standing outside herself, watching the scene unfold in slow motion like a movie. Kerri reached inside her coat. Nina's mouth opened and formed a soundless *no.* Beside Nina, Elizabeth's hands flew to her face.

And then, in a split second that seemed to last forever, Kerri pulled out a gun. Gripping it in both her uncontrollably trembling hands, she aimed it straight at Nina.

Don't miss any of the titles in this terrific series:

1. COLLEGE GIRLS
2. LOVE, LIES AND JESSICA WAKEFIELD
3. WHAT YOUR PARENTS DON'T KNOW
4. ANYTHING FOR LOVE
5. A MARRIED WOMAN
6. THE LOVE OF HER LIFE
7. GOOD-BYE TO LOVE
8. HOME FOR CHRISTMAS
9. SORORITY SCANDAL
10. NO MEANS NO
11. TAKE BACK THE NIGHT
12. COLLEGE CRUISE
13. SS HEARTBREAK
14. SHIPBOARD WEDDING
15. BEHIND CLOSED DOORS
16. THE OTHER WOMAN
17. DEADLY ATTRACTION
18. BILLIE'S SECRET
19. BROKEN PROMISES, SHATTERED DREAMS
20. HERE COMES THE BRIDE
21. FOR THE LOVE OF RYAN
22. ELIZABETH'S SUMMER LOVE
23. SWEET KISS OF SUMMER
24. HIS SECRET PAST
25. BUSTED!
26. THE TRIAL OF JESSICA WAKEFIELD
27. ELIZABETH AND TODD FOREVER
28. ELIZABETH'S HEARTBREAK
29. ONE LAST KISS
31. THE TRUTH ABOUT RYAN
32. THE BOYS OF SUMMER
33. OUT OF THE PICTURE

THRILLERS
HE'S WATCHING YOU
KISS OF THE VAMPIRE
RUNNING FOR HER LIFE
THE HOUSE OF DEATH
THE ROOMMATE
WANTED FOR MURDER
WHAT WINSTON SAW
DEAD BEFORE DAWN
KILLER AT SEA

SWEET VALLEY UNIVERSITY

THRILLER EDITION

Channel X

Written by
Laurie John

Created by
FRANCINE PASCAL

BANTAM BOOKS
NEW YORK · TORONTO · LONDON · SYDNEY · AUCKLAND

SWEET VALLEY UNIVERSITY: CHANNEL X
A BANTAM BOOK : 0 553 50674 9

Originally published in U.S.A. by Bantam Books

First publication in Great Britain

PRINTING HISTORY
Bantam edition published 1998

Conceived by Francine Pascal

Produced by Daniel Weiss Associates, Inc.,
33 West 17th Street, New York, NY 10011

Bantam Books are published by Transworld Publishers Ltd,
61–63 Uxbridge Road, Ealing, London W5 5SA,
in Australia by Transworld Publishers (Australia) Pty Ltd,
15–25 Helles Avenue, Moorebank, NSW 2170,
and in New Zealand by Transworld Publishers (NZ) Ltd,
3 William Pickering Drive, Albany, Auckland.

Printed and bound in Great Britain by
Cox & Wyman Ltd, Reading, Berkshire.

Chapter One

"What do you mean, I never take you anywhere?" Bryan Nelson rolled his pale hazel eyes in exasperation. "You sound like a throwback from some 1950s sitcom. This is the nineties—why does it have to be *me* taking *you* somewhere?"

"OK, OK," Nina Harper amended, putting up her hands in protest. "It's not about you taking me out or me taking you out. It's just that we never *go* out, period. All we do is study. And maybe go get, like, a piece of pizza every once in a while."

A warm breeze rustled through the palm trees as Nina and Bryan strolled through the quad of Sweet Valley University, where they both were freshmen. It was a gorgeous, sunny southern California afternoon. The lawn was full of students sunbathing, playing Hacky Sack, or dozing off with forgotten textbooks over their faces.

Nina had been studying in the library for hours. But when she'd decided she couldn't stand another second cooped up inside, she'd called Bryan from the lobby and convinced him to meet her for a quick walk across campus before Bryan's Black Student Union meeting.

Now, as she walked hand in hand with her boyfriend, the afternoon sun warm on her face, Nina felt the stress of her heavy course load melting away from her. Nina wasn't the kind of woman who came to college just to party and meet guys; she was totally committed to her schoolwork. Even if her parents *hadn't* expected a lot from her—which they did—Nina still would have pushed herself to do her best. But these few stolen moments with Bryan made her realize how much she needed more mellow times to keep herself sane.

"I can't even remember the last time we just went for a walk across campus, much less out to dinner and a movie," Nina continued. "I think if I spend any more time in the library, I'll turn green."

Bryan tilted his head to one side and narrowed his eyes. "Hmmm . . . I don't know. I think that look could work for you. It might even start a trend—'geek chic.'"

"Oh, I'm sorry," Nina said sarcastically. "I thought you were my boyfriend, but I must have made a mistake. Have you seen him around any-where?" She shielded her eyes with her hand and pretended to scan the campus. "He looks a lot like you, but he doesn't make dumb jokes."

Bryan reached over and poked her in the ribs. Nina squealed and pushed his hand away. "No fair! Tickling is illegal."

Laughing, Bryan leaned down to give Nina a light kiss on her forehead. As Nina smiled up at him, a stray Frisbee sailed toward them and landed at Bryan's feet. He stopped to pick it up.

"So, this boyfriend of yours," Bryan began, straightening up with the Frisbee in hand. "How big a guy is he? You think I could take him?" He tossed the Frisbee back toward the blond surfer-dude type who'd thrown it.

"I think he could kick your butt," Nina said decisively, stifling a giggle.

"Well, then, it's no wonder I never take you anywhere," Bryan returned, flashing Nina one of his two-hundred-megawatt smiles. "I wouldn't want your boyfriend to catch us together."

Nina groaned loudly. "I should have known you'd find some lame excuse to weasel out of spending time with me."

Bryan kissed Nina on the cheek. "Don't even joke about that," he said softly. "You know there's nothing I'd rather do than spend time with you."

Nina flushed with pleasure, both at the kiss

3

and the sentiment. But she wasn't about to let Bryan off the hook that easily. "So how come we never go out anymore?" she persisted.

"Well, tomorrow night is karaoke night at Al's Bar and Grill," Bryan said, grinning. "We could get all dressed up and go there—I mean, I could *take you* there. I'm sure you'd be the belle of the, uh, bar and grill."

"Oh, puh-*leeze*." Nina punched his bicep playfully, then slipped her arm through his and pressed her cheek against his shoulder. "You know what I'm talking about, Bryan. One night out isn't going to fix things. I mean, we're both really busy and—"

"Completely broke," Bryan finished for her, his grin fading slightly. Bryan pulled his arm out from Nina's and looped it around her waist. "Listen, Nina, don't you think I'm painfully aware of the fact that I can't afford to take you out anywhere nice? I'd love to be able to do something really fun and exciting with you every weekend. But even if I had time to go out all night and sleep all day, which I *don't*, I couldn't afford to. And if I got a part-time or work-study job so I *could*, I'd have even less time to spend with you."

Nina sighed with frustration. "Yeah, and progressive woman though I am, I can't afford to pay any more than you can." She looked down at her sandals, her happy mood evaporating. While

4

Nina's parents were fairly well-off, they didn't shower her with fun money; they felt that college presented a good opportunity for Nina to make her own way and, in her father's words, "understand the value of a dollar bill." But at times like these, she wished *they'd* understand that without fun money, she couldn't really have any fun.

They walked for a few minutes in silence. Then Bryan squeezed Nina's shoulder, pulling her away from her thoughts. "Hey, look," he said excitedly, pointing to the large announcement board that lined one side of the main administration building. It was covered with papers.

"Why don't we check it out?" Bryan suggested. "Sometimes people who live near campus post flyers for baby-sitting jobs and stuff like that. Maybe we could find some part-time thing where we could make money and get some studying done at the same time."

Nina brightened. "That's a good idea. But I *do* have my doubts about my ability to study with a bunch of screaming kids around."

Bryan stopped walking and put his hands on Nina's shoulders. "Nina, you know how much I love you," he said in a low, husky voice that made Nina's heart beat faster. "There's nothing I wouldn't do to spend more time with you."

Nina tilted her head back as Bryan leaned in to kiss her. She reached up and ran her hands

5

over his dark curly hair. As his lips touched hers she felt a warm shiver run through her. *There's nothing I wouldn't do either,* Nina thought dreamily as their kiss deepened. *I know we'll find something perfect.*

"Roommate wanted . . . apartment share . . . apartment wanted . . . lost dog . . ."

Nina scanned the mass of flyers that were pinned to the student announcement board, absently twisting a strand of hair around her finger. "I haven't seen anything about part-time work. Oh, hey! Look at this."

Bryan glanced over to see Nina point excitedly at one of the flyers. For about the millionth time since they'd been dating, he realized how gorgeous Nina was and how lucky he was to have her. He still wasn't totally used to seeing her with her hair falling loose around her shoulders. Bryan had loved the braids she'd worn when they met and fell in love, but her new look was more sophisticated and, he thought, extremely sexy. In her pale yellow cotton sundress, its straps golden in the sun against her bare, dark shoulders, Nina seemed to radiate beauty and vitality.

"Hel-*lo*-o? Why are you staring at me?" Nina demanded. "Do I have something on my face?" She dabbed at her nose and mouth with the side of her hand, as if wiping off imaginary grime.

Bryan shook his head, smiling sheepishly. "No. Go on—what does it say?"

"'SVU Students: Earn Cash Just for Watching TV,'" Nina read. She turned and grinned triumphantly at Bryan. "That sounds better than screaming kids, doesn't it?"

Bryan whistled. "A *lot* better. In fact, it sounds perfect. Where's the fine print?" He joined Nina in front of the flyer. "'Students wanted for a psychology experiment involving the study of human responses to televised advertisements. Fifty dollars for each daily two-hour session,'" Bryan read aloud. "'Sign up at the psychology building, room 205.' Wow! That sounds like a painless way to make some good money. I wonder what the catch is."

"It *does* sound too good to be true," Nina said, her eyes sparkling. "It wouldn't even be like work! Not only would we be spending painless time together, but we could also go someplace nice for dinner *every* weekend with that kind of money."

"We could even afford to drive up the coast one week and have a romantic getaway at some little bed-and-breakfast," Bryan added, picturing himself and Nina curled up by a fireplace miles from the daily grind of campus life.

Bryan glanced at his watch. He had twenty minutes before his BSU meeting—just enough time to get over to the psych building and sign up for the experiment. "Sounds like a great deal to me. What do you say?"

Nina threw her arms around Bryan's neck and kissed him passionately. "I say let's go sign up right now. The librarians start to worry if I'm gone too long."

"Who *cares* whether people have brown eyes or blue eyes?" Nina groaned out loud. She put the cap back on her yellow marker and dropped it into the binding of her textbook. "I mean, what a totally useless and irrelevant thing to predict."

In the comfort of her Dickenson Hall dorm room Nina was trying to catch up on her biology reading. Usually she found the intricacies of genetics fascinating, but right now it was almost eight o'clock, she hadn't eaten dinner yet, and all the big *B*s and little *b*s that represented dominant and recessive traits were starting to swim before her eyes.

Nina leaned back in her desk chair and rubbed her shoulders, which were sore and tense from being hunched over her textbook all evening. It had been two days since she and Bryan had signed up for the psych experiment, and she'd gone through pretty much the same grueling routine as always—classes, studies, and meetings. She had talked to Bryan briefly that afternoon when she'd bumped into him in the chemistry building between classes, and he'd promised to call her later and make dinner plans. But now her stomach was growling, and she was getting slightly annoyed on top of it. Nina hated it when Bryan got so caught up in his work that he spaced on his plans with her.

Nina picked up the phone and dialed Bryan's number, but it was busy. Exasperated, she slammed down the phone, got up from her desk, and flopped onto her bed. *Who's he talking to?* Nina thought irritably.

She stared up at her poster of Maya Angelou, wondering if she should just head down to the snack bar and get a salad and a bagel. "I bet you wouldn't waste *your* time waiting around for some man," Nina said aloud to the poster. She studied Maya Angelou's intelligent face as if expecting her to respond. *Great—now I'm talking to inanimate objects,* Nina thought wryly. *I really need to get out more.*

Sighing, Nina rolled over onto her stomach and pillowed her head on her folded arms. Closing her eyes, Nina thought back to her conversation with Bryan on the quad two days before. Her heart still fluttered when she remembered the intensity in his voice. But so far it seemed as if nothing had changed. They still hadn't managed to find any real time for each other, and they still were broke.

But it's only been a couple of days, Nina re-minded herself, opening her eyes. *We took the first step when we signed up for that experiment.*

When she and Bryan had arrived at the psych building to enlist, they'd been more than a little nerve-racked. The screening process appeared to be a lot more competitive than they'd thought. There had already been an enormous list of names on the sign-up sheet; they'd also had to fill in a lengthy questionnaire about academic records and medical history. *It must be taking them a while to process all that information*, Nina speculated.

Nina heaved a sigh, hoisted herself off her bed, and went back to her desk chair. Picking up the phone, she hit redial. After two rings she heard, *"Hi, this is Bryan. I'm not here right now, but if you leave your name and number, I'll get back to you. Peace."*

Nina hung up the receiver, fuming. "You were there two minutes ago!" she yelled at the phone as if it were Bryan himself. It was one thing for her boyfriend to get caught up in his work and forget about dinner, but it was another thing en-tirely for him to make plans over the phone and rush out without even calling to invite her along.

As if in protest, the phone rang. *That'd better be him*, Nina hoped. She let it ring one more time before she picked up. After all, she didn't want it to seem as if she were waiting pathetically by the

10

phone or anything. "Hello?" she said casually.

"Hello, may I please speak to Nina Harper?" a young, friendly, and *unfamiliar* male voice asked.

"Speaking," Nina answered, curious in spite of her disappointment. "Who's calling?"

"This is Christian Jimenez from the SVU psychology department. I'm the graduate student who's assisting with experiment X212, the study of viewer response to televised advertisements. Congratulations, Nina. I'm happy to tell you that you've been selected to participate."

"Really? That's great!" Nina said excitedly. "When do I start?"

"You start tomorrow," Christian replied. "Sessions meet from two to four P.M. every weekday and this weekend too, I'm afraid. If you have a class during that time on any day, you may be excused from that day's session."

"That time's open for me," Nina remarked.

"Good. Now, you and the other participants will meet in room 302 of the main psych lab building. Please arrive fifteen minutes early tomorrow for a brief orientation—attendance is mandatory. The details of the experimental procedure will be explained, and then you'll view your first round of advertisements. After each session you'll receive fifty dollars in cash. Do you have any questions?"

"No! I—I think that's it," Nina said, trying to

11

contain the delight in her voice. "Thanks so much. Really."

"See you tomorrow, then. Good-bye, Nina."

"Good-bye." As Nina hung up the phone she leaned back in her chair and exhaled deeply. A huge grin spread across her face. She'd made it!

"Fifty bucks a day," Nina whispered. She'd be able to buy herself some new clothes. And she and Bryan would finally be able to afford to try some of the chic new restaurants near campus. Nina closed her eyes, picturing herself sailing into the posh Mountain Lodge Inn on Bryan's arm. She would be wearing a fabulous dress from Evita's, and Bryan would be looking dangerously handsome in his dark suit.

This extra money will make such an incredible difference in our lives, Nina thought, wanting to jump for joy. *If we save a little, we could even afford that weekend getaway Bryan was talking about.*

We? Nina's eyes flew open. She'd forgotten one important point. Just because she'd been chosen didn't mean Bryan had too.

What if he wasn't accepted? she wondered, a sinking feeling creeping over her. *That would definitely be weird.* After all, they'd done this in the first place to be together. And even though Bryan wasn't the he-man macho type, Nina knew he'd still feel uncomfortable if Nina could afford to take them out to expensive places and he

12

couldn't. *I'd feel the same way if I let Bryan pay my way all the time,* she admitted silently.

Shrugging helplessly, Nina put her elbows on her desk and focused her attention on the biology book before her, pushing thoughts of Bryan and the experiment out of her mind. Just as she was settling back into the rhythm of her reading, there was a knock at the door. Nina bolted up from her desk, simultaneously startled by the noise and thrilled to have an excuse to ignore biology. When she opened the door, she gasped.

Bryan stood in the doorway, a broad smile lighting his gorgeous face. His arms were laden with a large brown paper bag, a bottle of sparkling cider, and two plastic champagne glasses.

"Well, aren't you going to invite me in?" Bryan asked lightly.

"Oh—yeah!" Nina giggled and gestured Bryan inside, too astonished to say anything else. He strode past her and set everything down on her desk.

"I got us some gourmet sandwiches from that sandwich shop off campus you like. Smoked turkey and Brie, right?" Bryan took out two paper-wrapped bundles and a container of potato salad from the bag. "I'm sorry I didn't call before I came by, but I just had to run right out and see you when I got the phone call." He tossed some plastic forks onto the desk and gave Nina a sly smile.

"You got in too!" Nina shrieked. She jumped into Bryan's outstretched arms and planted a kiss on his lips. "I'm so excited. Can you believe it? Fifty bucks a day! *Cash!*"

"I know. I can't wait to start spending it on you." Bryan glanced down at the spread he'd brought over. "Oh, wait, I already did." He grinned. "Well, I'm starved. Should we eat?"

Nina put her arms around Bryan's waist and slid her hands under his white cotton T-shirt. "Not so fast. I just want to savor this moment for a little while."

"No argument here." Bryan bent his head to Nina's neck and trailed a line of soft kisses along her collarbone.

"This experiment is like a dream come true," Nina murmured happily.

"I was so worried we weren't going to get in," Bryan admitted. Tenderly he traced the line of Nina's cheekbone with his index finger. "When the guy called, I couldn't believe it. I had to come see you right away so it would sink in."

"And is it sinking in?" Nina whispered. She slid her hands out from under Bryan's shirt and wrapped her arms around his neck.

"I don't know," Bryan answered, crushing Nina close to him. "I might need a little more convincing."

As Bryan pressed his lips to hers, Nina's heart

14

was so full, she felt as if it would burst. *How could I have thought that things were going bad between us?* she wondered dizzily. *From here on in, it's all good.*

"Are you sure this is room 302?" Nina asked. "It seems so tiny. I was expecting a huge lecture hall or something."

"Yeah, me too." Bryan scanned the small classroom from the doorway. There were about ten other students scattered throughout five rows of desks. A dark-haired girl and a long-haired guy with a goatee sat chatting in the front row. A tall, lanky guy with short dark hair sat off to the side, dozing off with his cheek resting against the chalkboard wall. The voices of the few students who sat talking echoed hollowly through the harshly fluorescent-lit space. A podium stood empty at the front of the room.

It seemed like an awfully small turnout, considering that the experiment was a great deal for anyone who was broke and liked to watch TV—which meant most if not all of the people Bryan knew on campus. "I guess the selection process was even tougher than we thought," Bryan mused. "We really *are* lucky we got in."

"Maybe it wasn't luck," Nina said. "Maybe it was our grades or something else on those forms we filled out." She nodded toward a pretty young woman with a blond ponytail sitting in the back row. "Hey, she's in my women's studies seminar. She seems really nice. Let's go sit with her."

The blonde looked up as Bryan and Nina approached. She had a warm, open smile and friendly gray eyes. "Women's studies, right?" she said to Nina. "I'm Kerri Drohan."

"Nina Harper." Nina extended her hand and took the nearest empty desk. "It's nice to meet you, Kerri."

"Don't believe her," Bryan warned Kerri teasingly as he sat down. "She just wants to use you for your class notes."

Kerri laughed.

Nina rolled her eyes. "This is my boyfriend, Bryan Nelson."

"Hey, Bryan." Kerri smiled warmly at him, then turned back to Nina. "I'm so glad to see someone I recognize here. Stuff like this always goes by faster if you have somebody to talk to. This experiment sounds pretty boring, but I *had* to sign up. My cash flow situation was calling for desperate measures, if you know what I mean."

"I *definitely* know what you mean," Nina agreed. "Watching ads on TV isn't really my idea of a good time. Plus if I even see a *picture* of a candy bar, I end up craving it for weeks. This has to be the worst possible thing I could do for my diet."

16

Bryan chuckled. Nina was always going on about watching her weight. He thought her tall, solidly built figure was heart stopping just the way it was, but early in their relationship he'd learned not to argue with her.

"Ugh, tell me about it!" Kerri groaned. "Practically every commercial shows you people stuffing their faces. After two hours I'll probably go on a major spree at the snack bar and have to spend all the money I make on larger-size pants."

Nina laughed. She opened her mouth as if to say something else, but suddenly her eyes flickered away from Kerri and her mouth just remained open. Bryan followed her gaze to the front of the room and felt a scowl cloud his features.

A tall, broad-chested young man in a lab coat was striding across the classroom toward the podium. His dark wavy hair fell into his electric green eyes.

Bryan felt a wave of annoyance crash over him as he turned his attention back to Nina. Judging from the dopey expression on her face, she was a sucker for a guy in a lab coat—or at least for *this* particular guy, with his chiseled, classic features and impressive build. Bryan didn't know much about what women considered attractive in men, but the fact that Lab Coat Boy looked as if he'd just stepped off the set of a nighttime soap opera strongly suggested that he was what was commonly known as a hunk.

17

As Bryan watched, glowering, Nina seemed to shake herself back to consciousness. She caught Bryan's eye and flashed him a contrite, embarrassed grin.

The sight of Nina's smile was almost enough to make Bryan let the whole thing go. It wasn't as if *he'd* never noticed an attractive woman while he'd been dating Nina, and that didn't make him love her any less. Still, it annoyed him that she'd been so blatant about it.

How would she *like it if I checked out another girl in front of* her? Bryan wondered, feeling his irritation mount. He deliberately looked away, refusing to meet Nina's gaze.

Her cheeks burning, Nina kicked herself mentally. What had come over her? She couldn't believe she'd panted like a puppy at that hot guy with Bryan sitting *right there.*

But that guy in the lab coat is movie star beautiful, she rationalized. *What woman could help herself?* Nina stole a glance at Kerri and felt validated to see that Kerri also appeared to be giving the gorgeous guy a thorough once-over. *We're only human, after all.*

Nina looked back at Bryan. His mouth was set in a tight line, and his eyes were focused toward the front of the room, where the guy had assumed the podium and was introducing himself as

Christian Jimenez. *He's the assistant who called me,* Nina realized. *So who's leading the experiment?*

Out of the corner of her eye she saw a figure enter the classroom. Turning her attention to the door, she saw a tall, gaunt, balding, middle-aged man with small, lined eyes, a drooping nose, and a meticulously trimmed black beard peppered with gray. As Nina watched, he quietly crossed the room behind Christian and flattened his back against the wall by the corner.

Christian extended his arm in the direction of the man in the corner, who seemed to narrow his eyes slightly. As everyone's attention turned toward him, the older man stretched his mouth into a grimace that he must have thought passed as a smile. His eyes darted from side to side as if he were looking for an escape route or simply couldn't bear to meet the students' eyes. Nina could practically feel the tension in his shoulders from her seat in the back of the room.

"And it is my privilege and pleasure to introduce Dr. Charles Akre, the professor conducting experiment X212," Christian announced. "I'm sure those of you with a background in psychology are familiar with his work."

So that's *Dr. Charles Akre!* For a second Nina forgot all about Bryan's jealousy. She stared at the nervous-looking man, who was still darting his eyes back and forth across the room. Dr. Akre was an eminent psychologist who had received several prestigious academic honors and been published in countless journals. Nina had read about several of his groundbreaking human behavior studies in Psychology 101. She'd wanted to sign up for one of his courses, but he taught very rarely and then only highly exclusive graduate-level seminars. It was exciting to be part of a project he was leading—even if the professor himself seemed a little standoffish. *Maybe he's one of those temperamental-genius types who doesn't deal well with people,* Nina reasoned, trying not to let Dr. Akre's chilly air dampen her enthusiasm.

"This experiment is funded by a private organization called EFC, which does market research for a number of advertising agencies."

Bryan felt torn as he tried to focus on Christian's words and ignore how Nina's eyes were burning into his face, searching for signs that he was ready to forgive her. Of course he knew she was here so they could spend time together, because they cared about each other. But somehow that just made her gawking at Christian all the more insulting.

"The project is designed to study human reactions to a variety of stimuli in advertisements in terms of brain activity and other physiological responses," Christian went on. "EFC will be using this information to help advertising agencies best serve consumers and create maximum effectiveness in their advertising campaigns. And we at the SVU psychology department will be learning about the response of the human mind to the kind of repetitive stimuli that most of us are bombarded with every day in this media-saturated age."

Bryan found it slightly odd that SVU would be taking money from ad agencies, even indirectly, to conduct scientific research. It almost sounded as if the experiment wasn't designed to further knowledge at all but simply to help advertisers sell products. *It seems pretty unethical,* Bryan admitted to himself. But he knew from his work with the BSU that SVU, like many universities, was in a major funding crunch. It was almost impossible for the school to provide grants for many of the student services and community programs that the university had prided itself upon. Who was he to say from whom the school should and shouldn't accept money? *After all, fifty dollars of that money is going into my pocket every day,* Bryan reminded himself. When he thought about it in those terms, the ethical issue had a funny way of seeming less important.

"And now I'm sure Dr. Akre would like to say a few words to you all," Christian concluded, turning his head toward the professor. Bryan, along with the rest of the students, looked expectantly toward Dr. Akre. For a moment the professor seemed to stiffen and shrink farther back into the corner. But he recovered almost instantly, managing a tight smile that gave the impression his lips had been ironed and starched, and walked slowly and purposefully toward the podium.

"Thank you, Mr. Jimenez," Dr. Akre said slowly and deliberately in a clipped voice bearing traces of an accent Bryan didn't recognize. His knuckles were white as he gripped the podium from either side. "It is my distinct pleasure to observe such a fine group of Sweet Valley University students in this, one of the most fascinating research projects I have had the honor of conducting."

He sure doesn't sound *pleased,* Bryan thought. In fact, if Dr. Akre's cold, impassive tone was concealing any kind of emotion, it was distaste . . . distaste for what or whom, Bryan wasn't sure. But he was sure of one thing: The professor's ultra-reserved demeanor creeped him out. He knew scientists were supposed to be neutral and unemotional, but he'd seen more warmth on the faces of mannequins in storefront windows than he saw on Dr. Akre's right now.

A sidelong glance at Nina's furrowed brow and troubled, quizzical expression told Bryan he wasn't alone. Bryan knew Nina was as concerned with ethics and principles as he was. He also knew from the guarded look on her usually open, expressive face that she was just as unnerved by Dr. Akre's clinical manner—maybe more.

For a second Bryan's annoyance washed away as a wave of protectiveness came over him. He hated to see Nina so full of trepidation. He had an overwhelming urge to take her hand in his and squeeze it, to give her the sign that all was forgiven and that they were in this together. After all, he trusted Nina completely. It wasn't as if their relationship were so fragile that it could be seriously affected by her looking at another guy.

Dr. Akre coughed into his hand. "And with that I will return the floor to my capable assistant, Mr. Jimenez, who will direct you to your cubicles so that the experiment may begin." The professor backed slowly across the room and into the corner again.

Bryan was about to take Nina's hand in his and give her a warm smile, but he blanched when her uneasy look vanished the moment Christian stepped up to the podium and began talking.

"Now, I'm sure you're all looking forward to watching some quality programming," Christian said with a grin.

Nina laughed, and the rest of Christian's words were drowned out by the echo of her laugh in Bryan's ears. Bryan folded his arms stiffly across his chest. Maybe he wasn't ready to forgive Nina yet.

As Bryan slouched down in his seat, fuming, he could feel Nina's eyes on him. *She must have noticed me tense up,* he thought, turning his head pointedly in the other direction and staring fixedly at the chalkboard on the wall. True, he was probably overreacting. He knew Nina loved him. But what self-respecting guy *would* react calmly to his girlfriend hanging on the every word of some guy who looked like he belonged in *Vanity Fair?*

I'll patch things up with Nina later, Bryan resolved. *But right now I think I'll let her sweat a little longer.*

Chapter Two

"Well, *this* is really romantic," Nina said aloud, her voice echoing across the bare walls of the tiny cubicle she had just entered. "I'm so glad Bryan and I found the *perfect* way to spend more time together."

After the orientation Christian had told the students that they would each be assigned to individual lab cubicles and that he would be coming around to each room to hook everyone up to the experimental equipment. Then he'd called out names and numbers, and the students had filed out into the hallway to their cubes. Bryan had bolted from the orientation room as soon as his assigned number was called, leaving Nina staring after him in amazement. She knew Bryan could be pretty stubborn when he wanted to be, but she couldn't believe he would let an innocent little look totally ruin his mood.

He knows it's him I love, Nina thought in

exasperation. *Otherwise why would I even* be *here? The point of doing this experiment was to strengthen our relationship, and now we're not even speaking to each other.* It would have been almost laughable if Nina hadn't felt so hurt and disappointed.

As she surveyed her cubicle the knot of disappointment in her stomach twisted into something more like apprehension. The space was a cramped, sterile square with bare cinder block walls and a cement floor. Fluorescent track lighting hung from the high ceiling, but the light it shed was absorbed almost entirely by the dark gray plaster surrounding it, giving the room a dim, cavelike feel. A large television was set into one wall so that only the screen was visible; Nina knew from the orientation that it was operated from the central control room on the other side of the wall. The TV screen shimmered silently with static, its glow dulled by its surroundings.

Facing the TV monitor, in the center of the room, was a metal chair with a rounded metal headset protruding from the back. Electrodes dangled from wires on the headset. A cord at the bottom of the headset led under the chair and into a slot in the wall just below the TV monitor. The whole apparatus reminded Nina of an electric chair.

"So how do you like your new home away from home?"

Nina whirled, startled, to see Christian standing in the doorway. His arms were folded against his broad chest, and he wore an apologetic grin.

"Pretty cozy, huh?" he added.

Nina forced a smile and waved her hand around the room dismissively. "A few posters, some throw rugs . . . this place has real potential."

Christian smiled warmly in response. "You don't sound too convinced."

"Well, it looks a little . . . I don't know." Nina searched her mind for the source of the creepy feeling the room gave her. "Like something out of *A Clockwork Orange*." She turned her eyes to Christian and gave him what she hoped was an I'm-a-good-sport grin. "I'm not going to get, like, *reconditioned* or anything, am I?"

Christian laughed. His laugh would have sent tingles up Nina's spine if she hadn't been so plagued with guilt every time she noticed how cute he was. "I know, you were picturing yourself sitting on a couch with a bowl of popcorn, right?"

"Sort of," Nina admitted, eyeing the torturous-looking metal chair with reluctance. She'd actually pictured herself and Bryan snuggled on a couch, feeding each other popcorn, but that didn't seem like an appropriate detail to share with Christian.

"I guess I have to take the blame for that," Christian confessed. "I mean, I did sort of gloss over the details when I printed up those flyers.

27

Honestly, would you have responded to an ad that read 'Earn Money Just for Watching Commercials with Electrodes Strapped to Your Head'?"

"I guess not." Nina let out a strangled little laugh.

Christian gave her another apologetic smile, meeting her eyes for a few lingering seconds this time. His open, friendly face—*Friendly*, Nina reminded herself, *not devastatingly gorgeous*—was almost enough to make her feel at ease. But as her eyes left Christian's and traveled the cinder block walls once again, coming to rest on the chair's metal headset and its tangled mass of wires, Nina felt the knot of fear in her stomach tighten.

"Well, shall we get started?" Christian asked with slightly forced-sounding brightness, gesturing for her to sit down.

Nina gulped before stepping gingerly over to the chair and lowering herself into it. As she leaned slowly back, trying to relax, the metal slats of the chair dug into her shoulder blades. Shifting uncomfortably, she blinked at the bright glow of the TV monitor that loomed before her, filling her vision completely. She hadn't realized how huge it was.

As Christian bent and began taping electrodes to her forehead and the pulse points along her collarbone, Nina fought to keep from squirming. It wasn't that the cool touch of his fingers was unpleasant, exactly. But with every wire Christian attached to her, Nina felt a little more like a caged animal. She found herself suddenly wondering where Bryan was. Which of the doorways she'd passed led to the cubicle where *he* was trapped? Did he feel as claustrophobic and weirded out as she did?

If only things were cool between Bryan and me, I wouldn't be so nervous, Nina thought ruefully. *I could make it through two hours of* anything *if I knew Bryan would be waiting for me with open arms when it was over.* But it didn't seem as if Bryan would be opening his arms to her anytime soon.

Nina knew she was in for some serious groveling when the session ended. She tried to console herself with the thought that making up from a fight with Bryan usually led to the two of them kissing so passionately they had to gasp for breath. But somehow, sitting in this cold cubicle with wires hooked up to her forehead and metal chair slats jabbing into her back, Nina found it almost impossible to conjure up the sensation of Bryan's lips on hers.

It's going to be a long two hours, she thought grimly as Christian taped the last electrode to her forehead.

"Honey, this tastes just like real cheese!" the middle-aged man exclaimed in a tone that was somewhere between booming and squealing.

His wife stretched her mouth into an impossibly wide, white-toothed grin and held up a small glass jar filled with a yellowish orange substance. "That's because it's made with *ten percent* real cheese, Bob!" she responded, sounding giddy with joy.

Bryan blinked his aching eyes and felt a tear slide down the side of his face. He wiped it away with his index finger. How long had he been staring at this screen?

This can't be good for my eyes, Bryan realized. Not to mention his neck and back, which were stiff from holding still to keep the electrodes from yanking loose.

In the past hour, or for however long he'd been sitting in this excruciating metal chair—it felt like days—Bryan had seen ads for everything from detergent to cars to frozen dinners to psychic hot lines. He'd learned how to keep his engine cleaner, his whites whiter, and his babies drier. All the bright, eye-catching colors were starting to blur before his eyes, and his ears were ringing with the catchy but oddly tuneless jingles that blared incessantly in his ears.

Why did I sign up for this thing again anyway? Bryan wondered to himself, fighting the urge to scratch frantically at the several itchy spots on his forehead.

On the TV screen a couple swathed in golden light clinked glasses by the fireplace as the names of the fifty greatest love songs of all time scrolled down the screen. *That's right—Nina,* Bryan recalled.

He tried to concentrate on the thought of getting fifty bucks a day in cash in the hopes of ignoring his itchy forehead. He remembered how great it had felt to see the look on Nina's face when he surprised her the other day with dinner. Once he had some cash, he'd be able to make more little romantic gestures like that.

One of the things he loved about Nina was that she was totally unimpressed by material things, but whenever he got her some little trinket or joke gift that showed her he'd been thinking of her, her face shone with so much love and gratitude that he'd think he had just given her the moon and stars. Thinking of Nina and her heart-melting smile, Bryan actually relaxed in his chair and forgot about the electrodes for a second.

The address and 800 number to order the greatest love songs two-CD set disappeared and was replaced by a gorgeous woman in a dramatically cut red dress on the arm of a tuxedoed young man. As the camera zoomed in on her she tossed her long dark hair over her shoulder. Then she took a lipstick from her purse, uncapped it, and ran it sexily along the contours of her already perfectly lined crimson mouth. Stretching her lips into a hypnotic smile, she batted her lashes sexily.

As the dark-haired woman pouted at the camera, her boyfriend a blur in the background, Bryan suddenly recalled the look on Nina's face as she had stared at Christian so unabashedly. A fresh wave of annoyance washed over him.

I can't believe I could forget even for a second how she was scoping him out right in front of me, Bryan fumed. *Here I am, daydreaming like a total sap about romantic things I could do for Nina, right after I caught her flirting in public like that. Man, that is really lame.*

The thought briefly occurred to Bryan that Nina hadn't really been *flirting*—she'd just looked at Christian, then caught herself after a moment. But he pushed it aside as the bombshell in the red dress blew a kiss at the camera while a husky voice-over pointed out that none of her Joie de Vivre brand lipstick had rubbed off on her hand. *That's not the point,* Bryan argued with himself. *If she loves me, she shouldn't even be looking at other guys.*

Bryan watched as the camera swung around to reveal a second tuxedoed young man lifting his hand in a pantomime of "catching" her kiss. Then the young woman reappeared, a smug smile playing at the corners of her mouth. The man stood beside her, looking away obliviously.

"Flirtation," a throaty voice-over breathed.

"The lipstick that gives you the love of your life . . . and more. Only from Joie de Vivre."

The smirk on the beautiful woman's face tugged at Bryan's heart. *The love of your life . . . and more,* he repeated silently, letting the words sink in. Maybe things between him and Nina were worse than he thought. Maybe it was more than a simple issue of making time for each other.

The ad ended, and another came on. Bryan tried to pay attention, but as images of happy, laughing couples flashed before him all he could think of was Nina looking at Christian . . . laughing with Christian. Gazing up at him with those adoring eyes.

On the screen a handsome young man swept a beautiful woman into his arms and dipped her down into a passionate kiss. Bryan felt his stomach lurch. For all he knew, Nina could be making out with Christian right now in one of these very cubicles.

No, that's ridiculous, he scolded himself. *Nina isn't like that.* Or was she? He hadn't thought she was the type to check out other guys while her boyfriend was sitting right beside her either. But she'd done that, hadn't she?

Sitting rigidly in the uncomfortable metal chair, clenching his hands into fists to keep from clawing the itchy electrodes off his forehead, Bryan felt his anger toward Nina mount. A little voice inside his head was telling him he should just let it go, that he was just obsessing because he was tense and irritable from being strapped into this chair and watching all these stupid ads. But as hard as he tried to put the whole thing in perspective, Bryan just couldn't shake his growing resentment toward Nina. The memory of her looking at Christian, the idea of her kissing Christian, felt like a stone lodged in his heart.

Maybe I'm not *being unreasonable,* Bryan thought. *Maybe this is the first time I've seen Nina for who she really is.*

Nina squinted in the bright light of the psych lab corridor as she emerged from her cubicle. She put her hand up to her face, both to shield her eyes and to scratch her itchy forehead. Nina exhaled and rolled her shoulders, trying to loosen the tension in her back. Her neck hadn't been this stiff since the time her high-school astronomy club had taken a thirty-hour bus trip to Cape Canaveral.

Other students were spilling out into the hallway, blinking and stretching. Some were rubbing their eyes, others scratching at blotchy red spots on their foreheads. Their jaws were all set grimly, and the tension in their bodies was almost palpable. *I guess everybody had to sit in those same metal chairs,* Nina thought. *Ugh. Did*

34

the psych department do some study or something that proved comfortable seating interferes with the scientific method?

Nina saw Kerri making her way down the hall, massaging the nape of her neck with her hand as she walked. Nina smiled, and Kerri smiled back. But her smile wasn't quite as warm and bright as it had been before the session.

"You look like you enjoyed that about as much as I did," Nina commented as she fell into step beside Kerri on the way back to the orientation room.

Kerri gave her a crooked grin. "It was pretty grueling, huh?"

"It's hard to believe that people probably watch that many commercials in a day without even thinking about it," Nina remarked. "I guess we shouldn't complain—at least we're getting paid to sit through that stuff."

"Yeah, but people who watch TV for free actually get to watch TV shows, not just ads," Kerri pointed out. "And they don't have to endure sitting through lots of tempting pictures of cheeseburgers and milk shakes and stuff—they can just change the channel."

"That *was* above and beyond what any dieter should be expected to endure." Nina smiled. Now that she had someone to commiserate with, she was feeling a little less creeped out by the whole experience. "Cruel and unusual."

Kerri laughed. "Right on both counts."

Nina giggled. Just then she caught sight of Bryan emerging from a cubicle a few yards down the long corridor. He turned and started walking ahead of Nina and Kerri, as if he hadn't seen them. "Hey, there's Bryan. I'm going to go catch up with him, OK?"

Kerri nodded and gave Nina a little see-you-later wave, and Nina took off in a sprint to catch up with Bryan.

"Hey, sweetie, how'd it go?" she called out cheerfully when she was a couple of paces behind him. She hoped she didn't sound fake, like she was making a point of trying to smooth things over. But that's exactly what she was trying to do.

Bryan turned his head and gave her a nod of acknowledgment but didn't slow his pace. Turning his head forward again, he mumbled something Nina couldn't catch.

"What?" Nina said brightly, pretending not to notice Bryan's cold shoulder. "Sorry, I didn't hear you."

"I said it was fine," Bryan said in a louder voice, still not turning to address her.

"Could you believe how dumb some of those ads were?" Nina persisted. Now she was sure her chipper tone sounded false—after all, it was. "I mean, that one for fake cheese. Have you ever seen anything so, so . . ."

36

Bryan paused in the entrance to the orientation room and stared at her with barely veiled annoyance.

"So . . . cheesy?" Nina finished lamely, looking hopefully up at Bryan. Usually when she made a dumb joke, Bryan would burst into laughter, throw his arm around her shoulders, and ask her what he was going to do with such a silly girlfriend. But Bryan just stared at Nina for a second as if she were beneath contempt. Then he rolled his eyes and went into the orientation room.

Nina felt her face burning with humiliation as she followed Bryan into the room and slid into the seat beside him. Bryan could be stubborn, but she'd never known him to hold a grudge over something so petty. Usually if he got annoyed with her, it was about something that really mattered to him, like missing an important BSU demonstration. Even then, he'd never stay angry long after she resorted to her desperate dumb-jokes tactics.

Hot tears welled up in Nina's eyes, but she willed herself to hold them back. *If anyone notices, maybe they'll think I'm just tearing up from staring at a TV screen for so long,* Nina thought miserably, staring down at her hands.

By now the rest of the students had filed into the room, none of them seeming as cheerful or relaxed as they had before the session. Nina looked up to see Christian striding through the open doorway, followed at a slower pace by Dr. Akre. She made sure her expression remained tense and exhausted so as not to throw gasoline on Bryan's fire.

As he took the podium Christian smiled at the weary-looking group of students scattered in the seats. "Well, I hope so far experiment X212 is everything each of you dreamed it would be. No, seriously, I'd like to thank you all for taking the time to help out with this project—I know there are probably more interesting things happening on campus."

A couple of students grunted and shifted in their seats. Nina let out a low sigh. *We want to get out of here already,* she thought, *not listen to you remind us how boring this was.*

"And with that said . . ." Christian reached into the breast pocket of the blazer he was wearing underneath his unbuttoned lab coat. He pulled out a thick white envelope and tore it open, revealing a thick stack of crisp bills. He held up the money and fanned through the bills with his thumb. "I hope these fifties will make your time here seem better spent. If you could all just form a line and try not to trample each other . . ."

His words were lost in the sound of chairs scraping against the floor as almost every student in the room bolted from his or her seat and surrounded the podium in what looked much more like a mob than a line. Nina, still in a daze over Bryan, was startled to find that she was the only one still in her chair.

Slowly she got up and approached the crowd of students. The faces that had been pinched with tension and restlessness a moment ago were now animated. A couple of guys in baseball caps whooped and slapped hands. Kerri, at the front of the throng, let out a little squeal of joy as Christian peeled off a bill from the stack and handed it to her.

Nina glanced over at Dr. Akre and was surprised to see him watching the group of students intently, his eyes narrowed. *I'm sorry, but world renowned or not, that guy gives me the creeps,* Nina thought with a shudder. She turned her attention back to the crowd around the podium before Dr. Akre could notice she was staring at him. Then her heart leaped wildly. Bryan was emerging from the throng of students, grasping his money in his fist . . . and he was smiling. To Nina's immense relief, he was still smiling as he met her eyes.

Nina took a deep breath. She had to clear the air now, when he was in a good mood. Maybe they could take their money and go someplace special to make up. "Bryan," she said softly, "I am so sorry. You know how much I love you. I didn't mean anything by it, I swear. It was just an innocent look. Can we please just forget about it?"

Bryan's gaze suddenly clouded over into a stare, and his jaw hardened. After a moment he said in a flat, cold voice, "I don't want to talk about it right now."

Nina felt her cheeks flame. *I can't believe he just shot me down like that again,* she thought, her patience with Bryan's jealous little snit rapidly running out. "Don't you think you've sulked long enough, Bryan?" she demanded. "I feel terrible, OK? Are we even yet?"

Bryan just looked at her and snorted.

"Fine." Nina fought to keep her voice down, but her hurt had turned to anger; she was practically seething now. Bryan was *way* out of line, and she wasn't going to stand there and take it from him any longer. *I'll just give him a little time to chill out,* Nina resolved. *I know Bryan will get over himself eventually.* "I guess I'll see you tomorrow, then," she told him lightly. "Right now I'm going to get my money."

Bryan gave Nina one last cold, hard look, then shrugged wordlessly and headed for the door.

Blinking back tears of rage and sadness, Nina stormed toward the front of the nearly empty room. *This isn't like Bryan at all,* she thought in confusion. *How could he be so cruel?*

As she held out her hand for her fifty-dollar bill, averting her eyes from Christian's sympathetic gaze, Nina felt herself shiver involuntarily. She'd been too focused on Bryan to notice before, but now she had the sudden uncomfortable awareness that Dr. Akre's hooded eyes were following her.

Chapter
Three

Tap, tap, tap.

Elizabeth Wakefield looked up with annoyance from the book of Romantic poetry she had been poring over.

Tap, tap, tap.

She sighed and closed her book. Elizabeth was a serious student, and literature had always been one of her favorite subjects, but for some strange reason she was having trouble concentrating on her English lit paper tonight. That strange reason was seated right across the library table, tapping a pencil against her teeth and drumming the fingers of her other hand against the tabletop as she read.

What is with *Nina tonight?* Elizabeth wondered. Nina was usually the one who insisted on studying in her own individual carrel so she wouldn't have to deal with any distractions. But tonight she'd suggested they sit at one of the long wooden tables frequented by the students who preferred whispering and giggling to hard-core cramming. Was she testing herself to see how many different repetitive actions she could perform simultaneously before driving Elizabeth to stab a pencil through her hand?

"Earth to the stress queen," Elizabeth said, kicking Nina lightly under the table. Nina looked up, startled. "I have a paper to write, and I can't form complex thoughts with all that tapping going on."

Nina dropped her pencil onto her book and heaved a sigh. "Sorry, Liz. I guess I'm just a lit-tle restless." She rubbed her eyes with the palms of her hands. "You know that experiment Bryan and I signed up for? We had the first ses-sion this afternoon."

"And? How was it?" Elizabeth's blue-green eyes softened. Nina had sounded so excited the day before when she had called to tell Elizabeth about her and Bryan's plan to earn extra cash. Now she sounded vaguely rattled.

"Well, first of all, I sat in an uncomfortable chair in a tiny cubicle with electrodes strapped to my head, watching commercials for two hours straight. So it's no big surprise that I'm having trouble sitting still. Second of all, Bryan and I . . ."

To Elizabeth's surprise, her best friend's eyes brimmed with tears.

"Hey, why don't we get out of here for a few minutes," Elizabeth suggested gently, reaching out to put her hand on Nina's arm. "We'll go get something to drink from the vending machine and you can tell me about it."

As Elizabeth and Nina sat holding cans of iced tea on the front steps of the library, Nina began filling Elizabeth in on the experiment and her fight with Bryan. It was a clear and mild evening, and the dusk sky was a deep, vibrant blue; Nina had relaxed visibly almost as soon as they'd gotten out into the fresh air.

"I just can't believe he was still sulking after the session." Nina was gazing off into the distance, looking deep in thought. "I can understand him feeling jealous for a few minutes, but it's not like Bryan at all to be so petty."

Elizabeth took a sip of her iced tea, then set it down on the step beside her. "It does seem a little excessive," she agreed. "Bryan strikes me as someone who's really secure in himself. I've never thought of him as the hyperpossessive type."

She had always liked Nina's boyfriend, largely because he was as principled and down-to-earth as Nina was—and she never saw him treat her with anything but love and respect. *It's so depressing to think that deep down, even the nicest guys are capable of that macho pride stuff,* Elizabeth thought sympathetically. *Nina's the most loyal person I know. She doesn't deserve that stupid jealous-boyfriend routine.*

Nina nodded. "He's never acted that way before. Bryan knows how much I love him. Why is he doing this?"

Elizabeth pulled the purple scrunchie from her long golden ponytail and twisted her hair into a loose bun. "I know it's easier said than done, but I wouldn't worry too much about it. Bryan is one of the more together people I know, and he really loves you." She fastened her bun in place and dropped her arms to her sides. "Let him sleep on it. He'll realize he was being a jerk, and everything will be all right between you two again."

"I guess," Nina said, sounding doubtful. "It's just . . ." She turned her face toward Elizabeth, her eyes questioning. "Do you think this whole experiment thing is a mistake? It seemed like the perfect way to make a fresh start in our relationship. But it's only been one day, and already things are worse than ever." Nina dropped her eyes to her lap, where she was nervously twisting a silver ring on her index finger. "At least when we didn't have time for each other, we didn't have time to fight."

Elizabeth frowned with concern. "But the first day of any new situation is stressful. And from the way you described the session, it sounds like even Mother Teresa would have been a little testy when she got out." She put her hand on Nina's shoulder and gave it a light squeeze of reassurance. "Seriously, Nina—don't get too worked up over it, or you might end up just making things worse. I'm sure everything will blow over by tomorrow."

"I guess," Nina said again, not looking up.

Elizabeth glanced at the glowing face of the clock tower on the SVU quad. She was worried about Nina, but if she didn't get started on her English lit paper soon, there was no way she would have it done on time. "Listen, I should really get back inside. But you know I'm around if you need to talk. In fact, Jessica's in Chicago at some convention, so you could even crash in my room if you don't feel like being alone."

Nina looked at Elizabeth quizzically, seeming to have forgotten her problems momentarily. "Wait, say that again. Jess is at a *convention*? Did I miss something? Did she, like, become a traveling salesperson?"

Elizabeth grinned. "Actually it's a national convention of Theta chapters." Elizabeth's identical twin sister, Jessica, was a member of Theta Alpha Theta, one of the most exclusive and prestigious sororities on campus—and, in Elizabeth's opinion, one of the snobbiest and shallowest.

"Jessica was babbling on and on about 'the empowering influence of sisterhood' when she called Mom and Dad to convince them to pay her airfare. But I have a sneaking suspicion that it's all a big excuse to go on a shopping spree with Lila and Isabella in uncharted territory. Jessica never leaves room in her suitcases unless she knows exactly what will be occupying that space on her return trip."

"We must warn Chicago," Nina said gravely. She held her hand up to her mouth as if it contained an invisible CB radio. "Chicago, do you read me? We have sorority sisters descending on the area in *T* minus five minutes. I repeat, sorority sisters in the area! Secure all mall zones!"

Elizabeth laughed, half with amusement and half with relief. "Sometimes I wonder if *you're* my *real* twin. Maybe you and Jess were switched at the hospital." It was a recurring joke between Elizabeth and Nina that though Elizabeth and Jessica were mirror images of each other on the surface, they were complete opposites on the inside. Personality-wise, Elizabeth had much more in common with Nina than with her own twin.

Nina laughed. She turned to look Elizabeth in the eyes, still smiling. "Liz, thanks for cheering me up. I'm sure you're right about Bryan—I should just stop freaking about it. He'll get over it."

Elizabeth noticed that Nina's voice wavered

slightly as she mentioned Bryan's name but chose not to bring it up. "I *know* I'm right," she said decisively as she and Nina picked up their cans of tea and stood up. After they walked back up the stairs Elizabeth tossed her almost empty can into the recycling bin outside the library doors. "Try not to even think about it until you see him tomorrow."

Nina dropped her can into the bin and sighed. "I'll do my best, Liz," she promised. "But chances are I'm not going to stop feeling queasy until Bryan and I have made up. This whole day was just too weird."

"Is your home being . . . invaded?" a deep, portentous voice intoned. On the screen, in grotesquely minute close-up, a gleaming brown-black cockroach scuttled across a sea of pristine white linoleum squares. That roach was followed by another and another and another, until the camera panned back to reveal a horrifyingly thick swarm of insects that covered half the floor and was growing fast. The sound track amplified the clicking, scraping noises of the thousands of tiny shells and legs as they advanced with excruciating defiance across the kitchen.

Bryan felt his skin crawl. He clenched his fists to keep from clawing at his forehead, where beads of sweat were pooling under the tightly taped electrodes. *Was it this hot in here yesterday?* he wondered. He felt as if he could hardly breathe in the warm, thick air of the tiny cubicle. He couldn't believe his heart could beat so quickly when he was just sitting still.

"Then smoke them out," the deep voice boomed as the kitchen filled with smoke. When it cleared, the camera zoomed in on the dead bodies of several cockroaches, their legs dangling feebly up into the air as the voice asserted that this brand was the fastest, most effective roach bomb on the market. "Kills them *dead*."

Bryan blinked. When he opened his eyes, the roaches had jarringly become glazed doughnuts with pink icing, nestled snugly together in a box lined with waxed paper. The camera panned out, revealing a red-pigtailed girl holding the box. With her free hand she took a doughnut daintily between her thumb and forefinger and sank her perfect, pearly little teeth into the pink frosting. As she beamed at the camera with a smile that was sugary in every way, Bryan found his mouth watering. *Mmm. I could really go for one of those doughnuts right now.*

Bryan blinked again. Even though the doughnuts looked delicious, he felt surprised to be craving one. *I can't believe I could have an appetite for sweets ten seconds after watching that gross roach commercial,* he mused. *I guess all these ads are getting to me.*

Bryan let out a sigh and tried to shift his weight in the metal chair without tugging the tape on his forehead. It was a skill he'd just about mastered in the past two days, though occasionally he still flinched at the painful sensation of fine hairs being yanked from his face. *Is fifty dollars really worth this torture?* Bryan wondered for the millionth time. As if the physical discomfort of the session wasn't bad enough, the boredom of watching commercials flicker before his eyes was causing his mind to wander onto topics he didn't particularly want to dwell on. Like Nina.

"Nina," Bryan whispered aloud, feeling a pang strike his heart. The moment he'd woken up that morning, Bryan had been overwhelmed with guilt over treating her so harshly. All day he'd been looking forward to seeing her and apologizing for being a world-class jerk. He'd planned to take Nina out to dinner that night so they could spend a romantic evening making up.

But as soon as he'd arrived at the psych lab Dr. Akre had appeared almost out of nowhere, as if he had materialized from out of the wall. He had addressed Bryan with more animation than Bryan had imagined him capable of. "If you're looking for Ms. Harper, she's in the capable hands of Mr. Jimenez. I believe he's hooking her up to the equipment as we speak."

Bryan had simply thanked him and headed

to his own cubicle in a daze. *Capable hands*—what had Dr. Akre meant by that? Was he hinting that something really *was* going on between Nina and Christian?

When Christian entered Bryan's cubicle a few minutes later to attach the electrodes, it was all Bryan could do not to reach up, grab Christian by the lapels of his lab coat, and tell him in no uncertain terms to keep his hands off his girlfriend.

Thinking of Christian and his smug I'm-getting-an-advanced-degree-and-I-happen-to-look-like-a-male-model smirk, Bryan felt his blood begin to boil. *I'd like to show* him *some capable hands,* he thought, clenching his own into fists. Everything had been fine between him and Nina before that pretty boy showed up on the scene.

Blinking, Bryan realized that the woman in red Joie de Vivre lipstick had appeared on the screen again. *Flirtation.* It was the first time Bryan remembered an ad repeating from the previous day. Again she ran the bloodred lipstick across her mouth in slow, hypnotic circles. Bryan felt himself growing more and more furious as he sat staring at the screen.

As much as Bryan resented Christian, he had to admit that it wasn't as if Christian had had to fall all over himself to get Nina's attention. Nina had been checking Christian out from the moment she saw him. If she was that flirtatious when Bryan was sitting right next to her, who knew what she did when he *wasn't* around? The more he thought about it, the more sure he felt that Nina was seeing Christian behind his back. She was probably with him right now, getting "hooked up."

Bryan exhaled slowly, trying to steady his heartbeat. He suppressed his urge to rip the electrodes from his forehead and run from the room. *I can't believe Nina could really blow off our relationship without a second thought to go fool around with that sleazeball. She's only known this guy two days!*

He closed his eyes. He couldn't think straight anymore. Was his jealousy making him totally unreasonable? Or was he seeing something in Nina he'd never noticed before?

When Bryan opened his eyes, a jowly middle-aged man on the TV screen was tearing a huge chunk off a plump chicken drumstick. As Bryan watched, the camera panned out to show a table heaped with buckets of chicken, mashed potatoes, gravy, peas, and biscuits. A hyperexcited male voice-over announced that if all this wasn't delivered in under thirty minutes, it was absolutely *free*.

"But remember, you don't have to *eat* it in under thirty minutes," the voice-over pointed out in a laughing tone. As he spoke, the man popped a biscuit into his mouth and started piling mashed potatoes onto his plate, still holding the half-eaten drumstick in his other hand. Bryan felt a strange mix of hunger and nausea as he watched the ad. The food looked delicious, but he was still too nagged with worry to have a real appetite.

Are they together right now? Bryan squeezed his eyes shut, trying to blot out the images in his mind. *Is he kissing her? Touching her?*

"Have you been injured in an accident?" a grave voice intoned. "Have you been the victim of medical malpractice . . . or marital infidelity?"

Bryan's eyes flew open. On the TV screen a man in a charcoal gray suit stood in a room that was supposed to resemble a mahogany-paneled library but looked more like a cardboard set wallpapered with pictures of books.

"Then the law firm of Slotnick, Meyers, and Platt can help you," the man continued gravely. "Hi, I'm Maynard Meyers. Our team of trained lawyers can help *you* get the justice you deserve."

The scene cut to a gray-haired man fixing earnest eyes on the camera. "My wife cheated on me behind my back for years, and I never suspected a thing," he confided in a forlorn voice. "Then she sued for divorce and tried to take me for all I'm worth. I was devastated—my life was falling apart. Slotnick, Meyers, and Platt helped *me* get what was coming to me. And they can help *you* too."

Never suspected a thing . . . devastated . . . , Bryan

repeated silently as a toll-free number flashed on the screen. *How could I have been such an idiot?*

His mind briefly raced through all he and Nina had been through together. He'd always felt that deep in his heart he could trust Nina with anything—that they were soul mates. But now, as he shifted restlessly in his seat, a voice in his head was telling him that he had no concrete reason to be so sure. Feeling wasn't the same as knowing. *It's not like* anybody *who gets two-timed sees it coming,* Bryan reminded himself. The Nina who was seeing Christian behind his back wasn't the Nina he knew at all. It was as if she'd suddenly become a stranger.

A new ad came on, for a fabulous cleaning product that made everything sparkle, shimmer, and shine. Bryan tried to block out the grating melody of its jingle so that he could think clearly. As hard as it was to admit, Bryan knew that he had two choices. He could convince himself that Nina could never betray him like that. Or he could start opening his eyes to the possibility that she could—and would.

And maybe already had.

Nina stood in the hallway of the psych lab, her arms folded tightly across her chest. She knew that if she let her hands drop to her sides, she'd end up biting her nails down to the quick.

Students were barreling past her, many emerging from psych classes and a few from the experiment. Most people were walking in groups of two or three, laughing and chatting, with backpacks and bags over their shoulders. But the faces Nina recognized from the experiment belonged to young men and women walking alone with their heads down. Their arms hung stiffly at their sides or were, like Nina's, folded across their chests. Obviously the strain of being cramped into the claustrophobic cubicles was taking its toll. By the time Christian had come into her room to unhook the electrodes, Nina herself had felt as if every muscle in her body were locked into one gigantic cramp.

As she scanned the crowd of students for a glimpse of Bryan, Nina wondered why she was so nervous. *It's just Bryan,* she reminded herself. *When have I ever felt uncomfortable talking to him? He loves me no matter what. Right?*

Nina suddenly realized that her left hand had snaked its way up to her mouth and she was unconsciously chewing on her thumbnail. She pulled her hand away from her mouth. *Get a grip, girl,* she chided herself mentally. *As soon as you see him, this whole thing will be cleared up.*

Just then Nina saw a familiar, handsome face emerge from around a corner of the corridor. Her heart did a little somersault in spite of her efforts to calm herself down. With damp palms Nina smoothed down the skirt of her ribbed black cotton dress. She'd chosen her outfit carefully—it never hurt to look nice when you were trying to get back on your boyfriend's good side. And she wanted to be dressed appropriately in case they went out for a reconciliation date.

As Bryan approached, Nina lifted her hand in greeting and pasted on a smile she hoped didn't betray her nervousness. "Bryan!" she called brightly, stepping in front of him. "What's up? I looked for you before the session, but I didn't see you."

Bryan stopped walking for a moment. He looked down at Nina, meeting her hopeful gaze. His expression was impossible to read. Then his eyes left her face and stared straight ahead. Without a word Bryan stoically stepped around Nina and resumed walking down the hall as if he hadn't even seen her.

For a minute Nina was too shocked to do anything but stand rooted to the spot. Then she whirled around and ran after Bryan. As she caught up with him she reached out and rested her hand gently on his arm. "Bryan, wait!" she begged. "This is crazy. We have to talk."

Bryan jerked his arm away as if Nina's touch burned him. His cold look made Nina shrink back fearfully. She opened her mouth to speak, but no words came out. Suddenly she had no idea what to say.

His eyes left Nina's face and traveled down her body, taking in her close-fitting dress. Nina held her breath.

When Bryan met her eyes again, there was a faint trace of a sneer on his face. "Who are you all dressed up for?" he asked in a cold, flat tone.

"For you!" Nina cried, hurt and indignation mingling in her voice. "Bryan, please, don't do this. I can't believe this whole stupid thing has dragged on for so long. I'm sorry, OK? Can't we at least talk about it?"

"What is there to talk about?" Bryan returned in a low, even voice. It sounded more like a statement than a question.

Nina gulped, blinking back tears. His icy tone was like a slap in her face. "Bryan, I am so sorry if I hurt you. But I can't make it up to you if you won't even talk to me." Ignoring Bryan's stony silence, she continued. "Our relationship is way too important for us not to be up front with each other. It's really hard for me to understand why my just looking at another guy is all of a sudden such a big deal to you. You have to trust me enough to tell me what's going on."

Nina gazed expectantly into Bryan's hazel eyes, looking for some sign that he knew she was right—that he even cared. *Please, Bryan,* she begged silently, *at least let me know that you still love me. It would mean the world to me.*

But Bryan just stared blankly back at her, his mouth set in a tight, hard line. Finally, after what seemed like an eternity, Bryan slowly shook his head. "I'm not so sure anymore," he said, his voice flat and emotionless. "I'm not sure I can trust you at all."

With that, Bryan turned and continued walking down the hall. This time Nina couldn't bring herself to go after him. She stood frozen in place, watching him disappear into the thinning crowd of students until her vision blurred with tears.

What did I do to deserve that? Nina wondered in bewilderment. *How could Bryan go from loving me to hating me?* She felt utterly devastated. Just days ago she'd been so excited and hopeful about their relationship . . . so sure, in her heart of hearts, that Bryan really cared.

How could the man I love turn into a stranger? Nina asked herself as tears streamed down her face. *How could I have been so wrong about us?*

Chapter Four

Don't look back, Bryan willed himself as he walked slowly and purposefully down the psych lab corridor, his hands thrust into the pockets of his brown suede jacket. *Don't let her get to you.* He could almost feel Nina's eyes boring into his back, staring at him with that look of sadness and disbelief he'd seen just before he turned away. It was so tempting to turn back around, take her into his arms, and promise her that everything was going to be all right.

I can't cave in just because she gives me that innocent act, Bryan reminded himself, steeling his heart. *If it's that easy for her to get what she wants, she'll just go on manipulating me.* A small voice in his head pointed out that the tears springing to Nina's eyes had looked totally sincere—not like manipulation at all. But Bryan didn't trust his instincts anymore; at least not when it came to Nina. She'd already proved herself capable of surprising him in a pretty harsh way.

As Bryan neared the door to the room where the students collected their cash, he was startled to notice that Dr. Akre was walking next to him, looking at him with an expression of sympathy and concern. *He must have seen me and Nina fighting*, Bryan realized. *Since he saw her with Christian before, he must know what's up.*

As he met Dr. Akre's gaze the professor gave him a crooked smile. Surprised, Bryan returned it.

"I saw what happened," Dr. Akre said in a hushed voice as they continued walking in step down the hallway. "I don't mean to pry, but I just have to say I feel for you—and I think you did the right thing."

"You do?" Bryan asked, unable to keep a startled tone out of his voice. The last thing he would have expected was for Dr. Akre to address him—or any of the students—voluntarily, much less to offer emotional support. "I mean, thank you, sir. Thank you very much."

"Don't mention it, Bryan." Dr. Akre smiled again. "You must always feel free to come and talk with me if you need someone to confide in. People like us have to—how do you say?—stick together."

" 'People like us'?" Bryan echoed, puzzled.

"Yes, Bryan." Dr. Akre studied Bryan's face for a

moment. "I noticed the moment I saw you that you had a rare spark of intelligence. Something like what ordinary people call genius. I believe that you have the potential to go far, Bryan . . . and whenever I see that potential, I do my best to nurture it."

"Wow," Bryan said, flabbergasted. "I really appreciate that, Dr. Akre."

"Anytime, Bryan," Dr. Akre answered, clapping Bryan on the shoulder. "I'm afraid I have to get back to the control room to make a few notes, but I'll see you tomorrow." They said good-bye, and Dr. Akre turned down a corridor.

It was so nice of him to say all that, Bryan reflected as he opened the door to the room where the students collected their money. *It's like he really wanted to* connect *with me.* Taken aback as he was, he felt grateful for the gesture of support.

And he really thinks I've got potential! The compliment, coming from such a distinguished man, meant a lot to Bryan . . . especially now, when his ego could use a little boost.

Bryan wondered if his initial reaction to the professor's cold demeanor had been unfair. *I guess my instincts about people haven't been too good lately,* he reminded himself. Dr. Akre had acted strangely during the orientation, but some people were just uncomfortable in group situations. Maybe under his stern exterior Dr. Akre was actually a pretty decent guy.

Nina swiped her meal card through the metal fixture beside the door to the dining hall. A light over the door flashed. Nina opened the door and entered the dining hall.

Ordinarily, if she was eating dinner alone, she'd just swing by the snack bar on her way back from class and pick up a salad to take back to her dorm room. But she'd spent most of the evening there already, crying her eyes out over Bryan, and she didn't think she could stand to stare at the same four walls anymore. Besides, whenever she was this upset, she needed a good, hot meal. Salad just didn't cut it as comfort food.

Nina picked up a tray from the stack by the dining hall entrance and headed over to the buffet line. As she slid her tray along the line she wrinkled her nose at the array of entrées: thick slabs of meat loaf the color and consistency of corkboard; stringy, dried-out spaghetti in a rapidly congealing cream sauce; viscous, grayish stew filled with chunks that reminded her of . . .

Nina shuddered. *Don't even go there*, she told herself, moving her tray farther down the line.

As she always did when she was depressed and confused, Nina felt a pang of homesickness. If only her family lived closer by, she'd have headed straight home and wheedled her mother into whipping up the ultimate comfort food: Mrs. Harper's baked macaroni and cheese. That dish had gotten Nina through many a high-school crisis. When it came to her mother's cooking, Nina was a firm believer in getting in touch with her inner child.

Nina looked back at the spaghetti and cream sauce, wondering if it was her safest bet. But she was distracted by a cluster of girls to her right who were giggling and pointing at something toward the end of the buffet line. Curious, Nina craned her head to see what they were looking at.

A young blond woman was pushing two trays down the line. Each tray was piled high with a jumble of food-heaped plates.

Nina did a double take. She knew that girl.

It was Kerri.

As Nina watched, Kerri grabbed a slice of meat loaf from one of the trays and crammed it, almost whole, into her mouth. With her free hand she continued to pull plates of food from the buffet. She tossed a dish of peas onto the top of one of her trays, where it teetered precariously. Peas spilled down from the dish onto other plates of food. Swallowing the last of the meat loaf, Kerri reached under the dish of peas and extracted a handful of spaghetti.

Nina put her hand to her mouth in shock as Kerri tilted her head back and stuffed her mouth full of spaghetti. The girls to Nina's right had stopped giggling and pointing and were now staring openmouthed. The scene Kerri was making was clearly beyond being funny.

When she finished her spaghetti, Kerri smacked her lips and vigorously licked the palms of her hands clean—*like an animal,* Nina thought with horror. Kerri pushed her overflowing trays a few inches farther down the line. Her eyes gleamed as she spied a wide, shallow tray of barbecued chicken. Reaching out with both hands, Kerri grabbed a drumstick and a breast. She brought both to her mouth and ripped a chunk from the drumstick, then the breast. Sauce coated her face, and scraps of food covered the front of her T-shirt. Kerri couldn't seem to eat quickly enough, tossing half-eaten chicken pieces to the floor and reaching out for more.

Nina couldn't believe her eyes. *Kerri seemed so nice and normal,* she marveled. *I can't believe she would do something like this in public.* Nina thought back to the way she and Kerri had joked at the first session about being tempted by ads for fattening foods. *But I thought she was just watching her weight, like me,* Nina thought with a twinge of guilt. *I would never have brought it up if I knew she had a real problem with food.*

Nina shook her head in sympathy. *I guess I shouldn't be all that surprised,* she reflected. *It's sad how many women have really severe body image problems.*

Still, it was odd that Kerri would be so public about her problem. Nina knew from her psychology courses that the vast majority of women who went on eating binges did so in secret and were deeply ashamed if anyone saw them gorging themselves. But Kerri didn't even seem to notice that a loose crowd of students had gathered behind her at a discreet distance, watching the spectacle she was making. It was as if she was oblivious to everything except the food in front of her.

Should I try to talk to her? Nina wondered. *Maybe this is some kind of cry for help.*

As Nina hesitated, fearful of approaching Kerri, a few of the food servers stationed behind the buffet line raced over. "Miss, please don't use your hands!" a middle-aged woman shouted at her. "I'm going to have to ask you to leave."

Kerri went on grabbing chicken legs and ravenously tearing bites out of them, oblivious to the stir around her.

A young male food server grabbed Kerri's wrist, causing her to drop the drumstick she was holding. Kerri looked up at him, her eyes wide with alarm, as if realizing for the first time that she wasn't alone. Uttering a strangled little cry, she struggled to wrench free of his grasp. As she writhed, her trays crashed to the floor, splattering food and ceramic shards all over the dining hall floor. Surprised, the young man let go of Kerri's wrist. As the room exploded into commotion Kerri darted through the crowd of students to the dessert table on the other side of the room.

Nina let out her breath slowly. She hadn't realized how long she'd been holding it. *There's no way I can talk to her,* Nina realized sadly. *She's way past the point of reason.*

Students were shrieking and picking food from their clothes. The sounds of other dishes clattering to the floor echoed through the dining hall. Food servers were pushing past the students, racing to get to Kerri before she could do any more damage. But Nina stood rooted in place, her gaze fixed on Kerri.

As Kerri grabbed a frosted doughnut from the dessert table and sank her teeth into it, an expression of something like pure rapture on her face, Nina had a strange feeling of déjà vu. Where had she seen that image before?

In the commercial, Nina remembered suddenly. *The little girl biting into the doughnut!*

Her mind ran through the other ads she'd watched that day at the session. She'd been too worried about Bryan to pay much attention, but a few distinct images stood out in her mind. She recalled the plump man gorging himself on chicken. *Could watching all those ads for food have set off Kerri's binge?* Nina wondered. It was

66

certainly understandable that being bombarded with tempting images of food would strongly affect someone with serious eating issues.

The cafeteria workers had managed to grab Kerri by the arms and were leading her toward the exit. Kerri's face was smeared with barbecue sauce and pink icing. Her eyes were as round as saucers and full of fear. She looked dazed, as if she had no idea where she was or how she had gotten there.

Nina shuddered. After her confrontation with Bryan, seeing Kerri like that was more than she could take.

Leaving her empty tray behind, she turned and quickly left the dining hall. She didn't want to see Kerri be dragged out like a rabid animal. And besides, Nina had lost her appetite. Comfort food suddenly didn't seem like it would be enough to comfort her.

Elizabeth glanced at the glowing face of her watch as she pushed open the front door of Dickenson Hall. It was a few minutes after seven—she had more than enough time to look over the final draft of her English lit paper and check her references.

Elizabeth slipped her free arm through the strap of her backpack. *I'm going to get a hernia from carrying this laptop back and forth to the library,* she thought wryly as she wriggled her shoulders to distribute the backpack's weight. *I wish I was one of those people who could get any work done in their room*. Even though Jessica, Elizabeth's number-one distraction, was out of town, Elizabeth felt as if her twin's energy lingered in the room they shared—after all, most of Jessica's clothes were still strewn around her side of the room from her flurry of last minute packing. And anyone who knew Jessica knew that her energy was opposed to studying of any kind.

Still, the room feels empty without Jess. That's probably the real reason I can't get any work done there, Elizabeth realized. She found herself hoping Nina would be in her usual carrel at the library and provide just a *little* distraction from English lit. Without her sister around, Elizabeth missed having someone to unload with after classes. Besides, she wanted to make sure Nina had worked everything out with Bryan.

The night was clear; the oval, almost full moon shone brilliantly against the clear sapphire sky. A cool breeze made Elizabeth shiver in her worn T-shirt and lightweight blue cotton drawstring pants. She quickened her pace, wishing she'd thought to bring a sweater. It was so stuffy in the dorm that she never remembered how cool it could get at night.

As she rounded the corner of the mathematics building Elizabeth felt her skin prickle, and not just from the chilly night air. Out of the corner of her eye she caught a flicker of movement in the bushes by the wall. The hedges were set back from the path where students walked, and the rustle she heard was much too loud to have been made by a squirrel.

Elizabeth held her breath. Did she dare look over to see what it was? Or should she just keep walking and pray that whatever it was didn't notice her?

A low, agonized groan from the bushes made Elizabeth's heart begin to pound. She risked a glance to her side.

At first she didn't see anything but a wildly waving shadow looming huge against the brick wall of the mathematics building. Then her vision adjusted slightly, and Elizabeth could make out a human form. The darkness hid his features, but the figure looked to be a young man, probably a student. He was tall and lanky, and his long limbs were shaking in a frenzied motion. *He's scratching himself*, Elizabeth realized. Even in the shadows she could see that one forearm was streaked with parallel lines. He must have scratched his arms until they'd bled.

Elizabeth didn't want to stare. She fixed her gaze firmly forward and kept walking, and in a few seconds she had passed the guy. The library was just past another row of buildings—in no time at all she'd be sitting in a warm, brightly lit room wondering if she'd imagined this whole thing.

Behind her Elizabeth heard another low, almost animal moan, which grew steadily louder. Then suddenly the voice broke into speech.

"Get them off me! Get them off, get them off!" The voice was shrill, agonized, and panicked at once; if it hadn't been repeating the same words over and over, Elizabeth wasn't sure she'd have understood.

Reflexively she turned around and took a step forward, ready to help the guy in whatever way she could. No matter how creepy the scratching and strange noises seemed, Elizabeth Wakefield's conscience wouldn't let her just turn her back on such a desperate plea. *I'll just find out what's up, get him some help, and go about my business to the library,* Elizabeth reasoned, trying to calm the pounding of her heart and the little voice that told her attractive young women shouldn't necessarily stop to help men who were screaming and clawing at themselves in the dark.

As she approached, the young man lifted his head and stared straight at Elizabeth with an expression of anguish.

Elizabeth froze in her tracks, terror trickling down her spine. She could see that his face, like his arms, was streaked with blood. As his bloodshot eyes scanned her face, not quite focusing, he

70

stretched out his arms, as if reaching for her. Another low moan escaped his lips, and he staggered forward a few steps.

He's coming after me! Elizabeth realized, panic catapulting her into motion. She spun on her heel and started running away, expecting to hear the pounding of footsteps behind her. When she heard nothing, she slowed her pace and risked looking around.

The guy was still rooted in place, staring blankly toward the spot where Elizabeth had been standing, his bloody arms outstretched in a pitiful gesture.

He wasn't calling out to me at all, Elizabeth realized, her adrenaline rush subsiding into a queasy feeling. *He didn't even see me—he was looking right through me.* She should have been relieved, but she just felt even more frightened.

As Elizabeth watched from a few paces away the guy let out another piercing shriek. Then he doubled over, wildly clawing at his back with both hands. His face was practically buried in a hedge. His shrill cry still echoed across the campus: "Get them off me! *Get them off!*" But even in the darkness, even from where she was standing, Elizabeth could see that there was nothing there.

For a moment she hesitated, unsure if she should still try to get the guy some help. As Elizabeth hovered uncertainly a few feet away, the young man continued to rant and whimper. "Get them off—smoke them out—they're . . ."

This guy is obviously on some major drugs, she thought grimly. *It's sad that he wants to throw his mind away like that—but that doesn't mean it's my problem.* If the guy was on a powerful hallucinogenic, there was no telling what kind of crazy, violent behavior he was capable of.

I definitely *better not get involved,* Elizabeth concluded. *There's no point in putting myself at risk to help somebody who doesn't want to help themselves.*

As she turned on her heel Elizabeth realized that the guy had crashed to the ground by the hedges and was lying curled in a fetal position. His legs kicked out spastically while his arms continued to scratch and claw at his face and torso. Elizabeth shuddered as she resumed her brisk pace toward the library.

When she'd left the druggie safely behind her, Elizabeth let out her breath with relief. But as she continued across campus she couldn't shake the unnerving feeling seeping into her bones. Maybe she was naive, but it was disturbing to realize that there were such hard-core drugs floating around on campus.

I guess there are always sleazy drug dealers around, ready to make money off college kids, Elizabeth thought. *Depressing, but true.* Elizabeth was a reporter for WSVU, Sweet Valley University's campus

TV station, and she had a pretty good sense of the issues facing the college community. She knew that drug use on campus, while tragic, was nothing new.

So why did that incident freak me out so much?

"It slices, it dices, it juliennes, and it will not rust, chip, dull, break, or wear out!" a fortyish man in a garish patterned sweater announced in one breath. His chipper, pasted-on smile contrasted strangely to the huge, gleaming butcher knife he held up next to his face. "The sharpening kit and lifetime warranty are included absolutely *free* of charge!"

Strapped into the uncomfortable metal chair, Bryan gritted his teeth as the TV screen zoomed in on the blade cutting through a large tin can. The harsh, rasping sound of metal sawing metal stood Bryan's hair on end. *I don't know how much more of this I can take,* he thought irritably.

"Now watch as it miraculously slices through a tomato in one stroke!" the man in the sweater exclaimed gleefully as he lifted the knife over his head. For an instant the silver blade reflected the bright lights of the TV studio. Then the knife came down, swiftly hacking a tomato into two pieces. The crack of the knife hitting the wooden cutting board was so loud that Bryan jumped, then flinched as the sudden movement tugged at the electrodes taped to his forehead.

"*Now* how much would you pay?" the man on-screen demanded.

Bryan's head throbbed. He was starting to get really impatient now. It was sheer torture to be strapped in this tiny room watching this drivel.

Suddenly the screen grew dark. A smartly dressed woman was walking down an alleyway, her heels clicking on the stone ominously. She screamed as a man jumped out of the shadows and held a knife to her throat. The scene paused as a deep, take-charge female voice bellowed, "Women! Don't let fear follow you down the streets!"

Bryan's eyes widened in amazement as the woman suddenly elbowed her attacker in the ribs and flipped him over onto his back. After the act was replayed in slow motion, the scene dissolved to a karate studio, where a muscular woman pointed her finger toward the screen challengingly while a dozen other women punched, kicked, and flipped male dummies behind her. "Here at the Tiger Ferguson School of Self-defense, I'll teach you the skills you need to . . ."

"*Get them before they get you!*" the women cried in unison, throwing their fists in the air before going back to battering the dummies.

Bryan pulled at his collar and cleared his throat. *There's not enough air in here,* he realized suddenly. *It's so stuffy—I can hardly breathe.*

Just then he noticed that a house consumed by flames had appeared on the screen. As the camera slowly zoomed in on the blazing building Bryan's face broke out in beads of sweat. *So hot in here*, he thought dazedly.

"The owners of this house will have to start over," a deep, gravelly voice-over commented. "Their entire lives have just been burned to the ground. Just lighting one match was all it took."

For a minute Bryan stared at the burning house, hypnotized. *Start over . . . lives . . . burned to the ground . . .* The words tumbled around in his mind. Watching the flames rise higher into the night sky, Bryan felt anger suddenly bubble up in him.

That's exactly how I feel . . . my whole life's been burned away! he fumed silently. *I came here to be with Nina, but that part of my life is gone now. There's no reason for me to be trapped here like a lab rat, but I have nowhere else to go. Look at me sitting here like an idiot, strapped helplessly into this chair while Nina is off somewhere with Christian, doing . . .*

Don't think about it, Bryan commanded himself. *Don't even think about her ever again after the way she betrayed you.*

"*Don't* let this happen to you," the voice-over urged sternly. "Sloan Home Insurance can help you make sure *your* dreams don't turn to ashes."

As Bryan stared at the fire that still filled the screen, the corners of his vision blurred with fury. All at once he couldn't stand being strapped into this torture chamber a second longer. Ignoring the pinching of the tape, Bryan reached up and began pulling at the electrodes on his forehead. *Have to get free,* he thought wildly. *Have to get out of here.* But the electrodes were attached more firmly than he'd thought. Frantically Bryan started to claw at the tape that held them on his hot forehead.

"Come on down!" a loud, nasal male voice bellowed from the TV, so loudly that Bryan's hand flew away from his forehead.

On the screen a portly, red-faced man with dark curly hair was practically pressing his face to the camera and screaming at the top of his lungs. "Bargain Barn is cleaning house with prices that are lower than the lowest prices you've ever imagined in your wildest dreams! We are *slashing* prices on furniture, men's and women's clothing, toys, electronics, fine jewelry, and hunting rifles!"

The monitor flashed to an overhead view of a large, high-ceilinged warehouse heavily stocked with merchandise. As the image moved at double speed, tiny figures scuttled around the store, picking up merchandise from the shelves.

As the time-lapse filming continued, the warehouse was stripped down to a vast, bare space with white walls and a gray floor. The sight of all that open, uncluttered space was incredibly soothing. For a moment Bryan's rage subsided, and he settled back into his seat. He could almost breathe easily.

"That's right, folks—come down here and *clean us out,*" the curly-haired guy barked, popping back into the frame. "We won't rest until every item is stripped from these shelves to make room for brand-new merchandise! Everything must go—that's right, *everything must go!* Our prices are so low, it is *in*-sane!"

Bryan stared transfixed at the screen, his fists clenched so tightly that his nails dug into his palms. He didn't exactly understand why, but the sight of the guy on the screen, the noxious sound of his voice, had raised his fury to a fever pitch.

"Everything must go," he repeated in a whisper, bobbing his head to the rhythm of the words. "Clean us out. Everything must go." Some sixth sense told him there was a hidden message in the commercial, but he couldn't decipher its secret meaning. He just knew it had felt good to watch everything get stripped away like that. "Everything must go," Bryan hissed again, still staring at the screen. Now the roaches he'd seen yesterday were crawling across the floor again.

The pressure in his head grew so intense that

Bryan couldn't move. He wanted to bolt from his seat, but he was frozen in place.

As he watched the roaches creep across the floor, his vision blurred again. Then it clouded over in a wash of red. Bryan was completely blinded—all he saw was red, filling his senses, feeding his rage.

The pressure became unbearable, and Bryan thrashed his head from side to side, moaning in agony. He kicked out with his legs and yanked again at the electrodes on his forehead. "Make it stop!" he screeched as loud as he could, still blinded by the wave of scarlet. "I can't take it anymore! I can't take the pain!"

But as he twisted helplessly in his chair Bryan felt the red close in around him, swallowing him up. The scent of the red filled his nostrils; he could feel its sticky touch beneath his fingers as the roach commercial voice-over blared, "Kills them *dead*." At that moment the red rage was all that existed.

Have to make it go away, Bryan thought feverishly, too choked by red to scream. *Burn it away. Clean it out. Kill it dead. Everything must go!*

Baldness is commonly believed to be a trait inherited via the mother's side of the family. . . .
Alone in her carrel at the library, Nina blinked back tears. The words in her biology book reminded

her of how she always used to tease Bryan—who, like most guys Nina knew, was terrified of the prospect of growing bald—by pretending that she noticed his hairline receding. Then they'd playfully talk about what it would be like when they were an old married couple.

Just remembering how it felt to joke with Bryan like that made Nina's eyes fill with tears. They had always had enough trust in their relationship to tease each other mercilessly without either one of them ever feeling hurt. A tear slid down Nina's face. How had all of that trust been shattered in mere days?

Nina angrily wiped the tear away. *I can't believe even biology chokes me up. I am really losing it over Bryan.*

She slammed the textbook shut with more force than she'd intended. The sudden noise made her jump. Out of the corner of her eye Nina saw a couple of students in adjacent carrels crane their heads around to glare.

Nina rubbed her eyes, which ached from crying, from studying, and from her third straight day of sitting through two hours of commercials. As soon as she took her hands from her face a fresh round of tears sprang up. The day's session had strained more than just her eyes.

Bryan had avoided her completely; he'd been gone by the time Nina emerged from her cubicle.

And the other experiment subjects had seemed even more tense than she felt—as they stood in line to collect their money the room was silent except for the shuffle of feet. Nobody spoke or smiled. Kerri was looking zoned out and licking her lips nervously; Nina couldn't summon the strength to approach her about last night's incident at the dining hall.

The tall guy who'd slept through the orientation had appeared especially drawn and haggard. Nina wouldn't have been a bit surprised if he hadn't slept since that first day. As he'd passed by Nina on his way out of the psych lab she'd stifled a gasp at the sight of jagged red scratches streaking his face and running along the length of his arms. Like Kerri, he looked strangely absent, as if the light of consciousness had gone out of his eyes. Nina felt sick at the memory.

Suddenly the carrel felt unbearably small and confined. Taking care not to make any more sudden noises, Nina pushed her chair back slowly and got up. Her cheeks were flushed and hot from crying; she needed to go to the bathroom and splash some cold water on her face.

As she walked down the corridor of the library toward the rest rooms Nina couldn't stop turning over the day's session in her mind. *Everyone,* not just Bryan, had been acting so weird.

True, the conditions of the experiment were

uncomfortable. And Nina had to admit that some of the ads the students had been shown were pretty creepy. That one with all the roaches crawling across the floor had appeared five times over the past couple of sessions, and it made Nina's skin crawl every time. And some of the new ads they'd seen, like the one for home owners' insurance, seemed strangely *off* somehow.

There's something weird about a commercial showing all that footage of a house burning, Nina reflected, thinking back. *It made the fire seem like a cool special-effects sequence in an action movie. Almost as if they were trying to glorify it.*

But still, Nina argued with herself, *it's not like the strange ads explain why everybody is so totally tense. You'd think people would try to have a sense of humor about it.*

Weary gloom coursed through Nina's veins at the thought. Kerri had had a sense of humor at first, but Nina had seen how totally unhinged the poor woman could become. Now Kerri seemed . . . different somehow. And Bryan—Bryan was practically a stranger.

A strange, nonsensical thought began to form in Nina's head. *Is the experiment . . . changing people?*

Nina shook her head in protest. *That's impossible,* she told herself. *All we've done is watch*

TV. *People are suggestible to the media, but not* that *suggestible.*

Besides, the tension between her and Bryan had started at orientation. And Bryan's jealousy of Christian had nothing to do with the experiment—it had nothing to do with *anything*. It just didn't make sense.

Nina pushed open the door to the ladies' room, still lost in thought. Sinks and a long mirror lined one side of the room, and a young woman was standing there fixing her makeup. Nina walked over to a sink several feet away, keeping her eyes down to hide the fact that she'd been crying. She turned on the cold water and bent over the sink, cupping water in her hands. After splashing the cool water over her face for several seconds, Nina straightened up and opened her eyes. She looked at her dripping face in the mirror, and unconsciously her eyes flicked over to the reflection of the other girl. Then she did a double take.

The young woman beside Nina wasn't just touching up her makeup. She was ringing her mouth over and over, in slow and deliberate circles, with a dark, creamy lipstick that already covered her mouth and most of her chin. Five shades of eye shadow streaked her forehead from her eyelids to her hairline, and her eyelashes were matted with black mascara. A stark ridge of caked-on foundation ran along her jawbone. Her shoulder-length, frizzy brown hair was snarled up with hair spray into a hideous wasp's nest, and her black shirt and jeans were smeared with lipstick and flecked with powder.

It took Nina a second to place the young woman under all the makeup. Then her heart sank.

She recognized the woman from the experiment.

Nina averted her eyes so the young woman wouldn't catch her staring. She reached down and turned off the water with a trembling hand. Stealing another glance up at the woman's reflection, she saw that there was no point in being discreet. *She has no idea I'm even in the room,* Nina realized. *She's totally in her own world.*

Nina tore her eyes away from the brunette's face and scanned the counter that ran along the mirror above the sinks. Cosmetic products were spread across the counter about a foot in either direction from the zombielike young woman. Bottles of loose powder and concealer lay spilled on their sides beside crushed lipsticks and dried-out mascara wands. The whole bizarre scene gave Nina chills.

As Nina watched, the girl suddenly stopped circling her mouth with the lipstick. With the same slow, deliberate motion, never taking her eyes off her own reflection, the young woman raised her other hand to her mouth. Then, stretching her painted mouth into a grotesque, clownlike smile, she touched her fingertips to her mouth and blew a kiss to her reflection.

Nina felt the same horrible sense of déjà vu she'd had while watching Kerri gorge herself at the cafeteria. *I've seen that before,* she realized, her nausea growing stronger.

Seemingly transfixed by her own image, the young woman continued to blow kisses to her reflection in the mirror. The lipstick slipped unnoticed from her other hand and rolled across the floor toward Nina. Nina looked down at the curly script on the lipstick tube.

Flirtation, she read. *By Joie de Vivre.*

Chapter Five

It figures that we'd get a heat wave the day I remember to dress warmly, Elizabeth thought. She stopped walking and shrugged off the red windbreaker she was wearing over her black denim overalls. *But I guess I did leave for the library earlier than usual tonight.* The late afternoon sun still glowed orange over the trees that lined the quad, veiled in a humid haze.

After her strange encounter last night Elizabeth didn't much feel like walking alone on campus after dark. Besides, she had a lot of reading to catch up on since she'd been concentrating on her paper for the last week.

Hopefully I'll run into Nina and we can walk back to Dickenson together, Elizabeth thought as she tied the windbreaker around her waist. *I still don't know how things went with her and Bryan the other day.* Elizabeth had stayed at the library until closing time the previous night to finish her paper, but she hadn't run into Nina. She hoped that meant Nina and Bryan had patched things up and gone out somewhere romantic together.

Elizabeth picked up her backpack and continued walking toward the library. Evening classes were letting out, and students streamed across the quad, talking and laughing. Elizabeth waved at a couple of people she knew from her classes.

As she approached the physics building on the far side of the quad, she saw a familiar figure emerge from its huge glass doors. It was Bryan. Elizabeth watched him walk slowly down the stairs of the physics building to the quad, then turn in her direction. As they drew closer to each other she saw that his hands were shoved into the pockets of his jeans. His shoulders were hunched, and his eyes darted worriedly from side to side as if he were afraid of something.

Elizabeth frowned slightly. *Maybe he and Nina* didn't *work everything out,* she speculated. Why else would Bryan look so unhappy?

When Bryan was a few feet away, Elizabeth waved at him and called out, "Hey, Bryan!"

Bryan jumped back, startled. Obviously he had been too preoccupied to notice her approaching. When he looked up at Elizabeth, his eyes were wide and unfocused. Then, after a second, the light of recognition dawned in his eyes. "Oh," he said in a choked voice, "Liz. Hi."

"I'm sorry I scared you," Elizabeth said with a nervous little laugh. Bryan seemed really out of it. Maybe his problems with Nina went deeper than she'd realized. "How's, uh, everything going?"

Bryan's expression was guarded. "Fine."

Elizabeth hesitated. "Are you sure? I mean, I don't mean to be nosy, but you seem pretty tense. Is anything wrong?"

"No," Bryan said through clenched teeth. "Everything is fine." He stared at Elizabeth as if he was hoping she would make her point and leave him alone.

Elizabeth's mouth opened and closed. She was utterly at a loss. Bryan had always been a good friend to her. He'd had arguments with Nina before—all healthy couples fought, in Elizabeth's opinion—but he'd never taken his anger out on Elizabeth. *Now I see why Nina was so worried,* she thought.

"Well, listen," Elizabeth began. "I'm not really sure what's going on with you and Nina, but just because I'm her friend doesn't mean I'm not your friend too. So if you ever want to talk—"

"Look," Bryan interrupted in a sharp voice that made Elizabeth catch her breath. His eyes were blazing. "I don't know what you want from me, but there's nothing to talk about." Bryan's voice, already quivering with anger, rose a notch. "Nothing, do you hear me?"

Elizabeth stared at him in shock. He was really scaring her now. "Bryan, I—"

"I don't want to hear it!" Bryan practically screamed. "You're just like she is. You want me to open up to you. Yeah, you'd like that. But I'm not going to fall for it, do you hear me?" At the sound of his voice a few passing students turned to stare.

"Bryan, please calm down," Elizabeth whispered. "I didn't mean . . ." She bit her lip. There was no point in arguing with him—he wasn't making any sense.

Bryan jabbed an accusatory finger toward her. "Just back off. I don't trust you, OK? You *or* Nina." His voice faltered at the mention of Nina's name. "I don't know who to trust anymore!"

Blinking back tears, Bryan looked away. For a moment Elizabeth thought she saw fear and confusion on his face. But when he turned back to Elizabeth, Bryan's eyes were hard. His tears were obviously tears of rage.

"Just stay away from me, and stop trying to pick my brain," Bryan said in a low, menacing voice. Then he stepped past Elizabeth and ran off.

Stunned, Elizabeth turned slowly around and watched Bryan's figure disappear behind a building. *That was more than a lovers' quarrel,* she realized with a sinking feeling. *Something is really, really wrong.*

Elizabeth shook her head in sad bewilderment. "Poor Nina," she said softly to herself.

Bearing down hard with her ballpoint pen, Nina traced the outline of a circle in the margin of her biology book. She sat slumped in her carrel with her chin propped in her hand, but she'd given up trying to study twenty minutes ago. Seeing that girl from the experiment in the bathroom had upset her too much. It was as if everyone around her had suddenly changed personalities.

Well, not everyone, Nina amended mentally. *Just everyone from the experiment.*

But it didn't make sense that the experiment would affect everyone so strongly. There had to be some logical explanation. Or, even more likely, a separate logical explanation for each incident. There was no reason Bryan's jealousy should have anything to do with Kerri's eating disorder or that either had anything to do with . . . whatever that girl was doing with all that makeup. It had to be a coincidence. All of it.

Nina dropped the ballpoint pen and buried her face in her hands. *Maybe it's me who's going crazy,* she thought miserably. The more she thought about the way Bryan was acting and the strange incidents she'd seen, the more it all seemed like some impossible figment of Nina's imagination. Nothing she'd seen fit with the Bryan she knew . . . or even with the little she knew about the other students in the experiment.

Suddenly a cold hand clamped down on Nina's shoulder. Startled, Nina jumped back so violently that her chair almost tipped backward. At the same time she uttered a strangled little cry and whirled around to find herself face-to-face with . . . Elizabeth Wakefield, who was staring at her with shock and concern.

Behind Elizabeth the students in the next row of carrels had all turned around in unison, like an annoyed chorus line, to glare at Nina. The girl in the carrel beside Nina craned her head all the way around to hiss, "If you're having trouble concentrating, maybe you should study somewhere else."

Nina felt her face flush with embarrassment and the adrenaline still coursing through her body from the unexpected touch. She looked up sheepishly at Elizabeth, who had recovered from her own surprise and was gesturing to Nina to come out of her carrel. Nina got up from her chair and followed Elizabeth out into the corridor. When the door to the study room had shut behind them, Nina exhaled slowly, trying to steady the pounding of her heart.

"I was about to ask you how you're doing,"

Elizabeth said in the light, cheerful tone that Nina knew meant she was concerned about something but didn't want to overreact. "But it looks like you've already answered my question. What's going on?"

"It's this new diet I'm trying," Nina said with a wry grimace. "The jump-out-of-your-skin diet. It really gets your heart rate up."

Elizabeth's laughter echoed through the hall, but there was a slightly forced note in it. "Come on, Nina, I know you'd never start a diet without making me join you. Don't forget our 'misery loves company' pact. Seriously, out with it. What's up?"

Nina heaved a sigh. "Well, you know how I told you about the experiment and how weird the vibe was at the lab?"

Elizabeth nodded.

"It's just gotten worse," Nina continued. "Everybody is acting really tense, and there have been . . . I've seen . . . I don't know. . . ." Nina trailed off, shaking her head sadly. How could she explain to Elizabeth what she'd seen?

Even I'm *not convinced that this whole thing isn't my imagination,* Nina realized. *If I tell Liz, she'll* definitely *think I'm insane.*

"People are just acting weird," she finished lamely. "And Bryan . . ."

Nina quickly filled Elizabeth in on the way

91

Bryan had been acting and the way he'd treated Nina when she'd tried to make up. "I don't know what to do anymore," she concluded, turning to Elizabeth with tear-filled eyes. "It's like he's not the same person."

Nina looked expectantly at Elizabeth and was surprised to find that her friend wasn't meeting her eyes. Instead Elizabeth was gazing at some point in the distance with a thoughtful expression on her face, almost as if Nina's words had reminded her of something. "Liz?" Nina asked, putting her hand on Elizabeth's shoulder. "What is it? Do you know what I'm talking about?"

Startled, Elizabeth opened her mouth hesitantly. Should she tell Nina about her run-in with Bryan?

It might make Nina feel better to know she's not imagining things, she reasoned, *that she's not the only one Bryan was lashing out at.* But then again, it might scare her even more.

"Liz?" Nina pressed. "What's going on? Have you seen it too?"

"I . . ." Elizabeth racked her brain.

"Tell me, Liz!" Nina exclaimed urgently. "Did something happen to you? Do you know something?" There was a strange, shrill note in her voice.

Elizabeth gaped. That was the second time in a few minutes that Nina had practically started bouncing off the walls with anxiety.

Elizabeth had never seen her friend so on edge.

I'd better not say anything about Bryan, Elizabeth decided quickly. *I can wait until she's calmer to bring it up.* Nina was obviously freaked out enough as it was. And it wasn't as if Elizabeth had any answers or explanations for her.

The thought of her strange confrontation with Bryan brought to Elizabeth's mind the image of the druggie she'd seen the other day. Somehow the two incidents were linked in her mind—it wasn't often Elizabeth had a bizarre encounter on the SVU quad, and now she'd had two in two days.

"I was just thinking about this odd thing that happened to me on campus yesterday," Elizabeth finally explained. "It really rattled me—when you were talking about the weird vibe going on at the lab, it reminded me." Briefly she described the obviously drugged-out student, screaming and clawing at himself. "It was the creepiest thing I've ever seen, Nina," Elizabeth recalled. "He had scratches all over his arms and face."

To Elizabeth's surprise, Nina's face went ashen. "What did he look like?" she breathed, almost in a whisper.

Elizabeth furrowed her brow. Nina's eyes were fixed on her with an urgent, almost pleading look.

"I'm not sure," Elizabeth said slowly. "I

93

know he was white, and kind of tall and skinny, and I think his hair was brown. But it was pretty dark out, and he was kind of bent over, so it was hard to see his face." She looked at Nina, who appeared to be lost in thought. "Why do you ask?" Elizabeth asked in what she hoped was a gentle, noninvasive tone.

Nina shook her head; the movement seemed to shake her back to the present. "No reason. It's just . . ." She spread her hands out helplessly. "It's weird, the way people are acting all of a sudden."

For a moment Nina looked as if she was going to say something else, but then she just looked down at her feet and shook her head again. Her arms dropped to her sides.

Elizabeth had never seen Nina look so at a loss. Her best friend was one of the most together people she knew, but now she looked small and confused. Elizabeth's heart went out to her.

Should I press her? Elizabeth wondered. *There's obviously something Nina's not telling me. She might feel better if she talks it out.*

But Nina wasn't the kind of person who needed to be coaxed out of her shell; her frankness was part of what Elizabeth loved about her best friend. Whenever Nina wanted Elizabeth's advice or support, she asked for it openly. *Maybe she's just not ready to talk about it,* Elizabeth concluded. *I'd better give her some time to calm down.*

"Listen," Elizabeth said warmly, slinging her arm around Nina's shoulders, "I know what you mean. There's definitely some weird energy on campus right now. Hey, the full moon is coming up." Elizabeth grinned at Nina, who she knew hated irrational, unscientific explanations of any kind. "But everybody will calm down eventually."

Elizabeth realized how vague and unhelpful she was being, but the truth was that she had no idea what to say. Ignoring Nina's glum silence, she went on. "I have an idea. We're both really stressed out. Why don't we just blow off studying for tonight, rent some movies, and go watch them in the TV lounge?"

Nina smiled wanly up at Elizabeth. "Thanks, Liz," she said in a shaky voice. "But I think I'm just going to go back to my room and try to get some reading done. I appreciate the offer, but I don't think I could stand to look at a TV screen right now."

Bryan rummaged through the top drawer of his bureau. Why did he have all these socks? Almost all of them were white sweat socks or black cotton socks. Why did he need so many of the same kind?

"One of each," Bryan mumbled, starting to throw pairs of socks into the large, half-filled trash bag in the center of his floor. Those red socks would have to go—all of a sudden Bryan *hated* those socks. He couldn't believe he had bought them. "What was I *thinking?*" he growled out loud. He separated the pair and tore each sock into strips before tossing them into the trash bag.

When there were only three pairs of socks left in the sock drawer, Bryan pushed the drawer back into the bureau with such force that the small alarm clock on top of the bureau fell to the floor with a crash. Bryan picked it up and threw it into the bag. He had a watch—he didn't need a clock.

He yanked his T-shirt drawer out of the bureau and overturned it, dumping its contents on the floor. Bryan got down on his knees and started sorting through the T-shirts, ripping apart the ones he didn't need anymore and throwing them into the bag. This was good. He was getting a lot done. His room was going to be really organized now.

It was around 3 A.M., according to the clock Bryan had just thrown away, and Bryan had been trying to study in his room since sundown. But he couldn't concentrate on anything; when he looked down at the pages of his textbooks, all he saw was red. His anger at Nina just kept rising up, choking him. He couldn't breathe. Bryan had gotten up from his desk and paced the room for a few hours before he started to feel like the walls were closing in on him.

The walls. Bryan got up from the floor where most of his T-shirts were in shreds and climbed up onto his bed. He began ripping down the posters that covered his walls, as well as the BSU flyers he'd saved to commemorate important events and rallies. Those times seemed far away now, like they were part of another life. The principles he believed so strongly in, that he'd worked so hard toward, seemed distant and unimportant. Nothing was as important as getting rid of all his excess baggage. All this . . . *stuff* that was confining him.

This room feels like a prison, Bryan thought for the fiftieth time. A fresh sweat beaded on his forehead as he tore feverishly at the Jimi Hendrix poster over his bed. "Everything must go," he muttered absently.

Bryan sighed with satisfaction when his walls were bare. All those pictures had been hurting his eyes. All those faces reflecting back at him, watching him. Now the walls reflected nothing but the harsh glare of the fluorescent overhead light. *It's so much better this way,* Bryan thought, feeling content for a fleeting moment. Then the anger came back.

Bryan returned to his bureau. He yanked out all three of the bottom drawers in succession, dumping their contents on the floor. Then he jumped back up on his bed. Bryan watched, exhilarated, as the top-heavy bureau teetered and then pitched forward, knocking a lamp off his nightstand. The lightbulb shattered, spraying glass across the floor, and Bryan felt joy bubble up in him.

Laughing like a child, he bounced up and down on the bed. It was as if he had been reborn. It felt so good to liberate himself from all this stuff. All the stuff fencing him in, trapping him.

Then Bryan felt the anger come over him again, like hands closing around his throat. He wasn't free, not yet. There was still so much to purge. He hopped down from the bed and grabbed the lamp that had fallen on the floor. Yanking the plug from the wall, he threw the lamp into the bulging trash bag. It was almost full—he'd have to make another run to the janitor's closet soon. But he couldn't leave yet, not with so much left to do.

"Still trapped," Bryan whispered to himself. "Still trapped." The phantom hands around his throat squeezed tighter, and Bryan felt his breath come in ragged gasps.

Bryan went over to the nightstand where the bureau had fallen. He saw that a glass of water had also been knocked over, leaving a puddle full of broken glass on the floor by his bed. Bryan bent down and picked up a handful of glass, not bothering to be careful of cutting himself. He could feel the shards slice into his palm but in a detached way, like it was happening to someone else.

Bryan threw the glass into the trash bag and wiped his bloody hand on his jeans leg. Looking back at the nightstand, he saw that a picture in an ornate silver frame lay facedown beside the corner of the overturned bureau.

Bryan picked up the picture and stared at it. It was a picture of Nina, taken not long after they'd first started dating. The glass over her face had cracked, but the image was still clear under the fine network of lines. She was laughing, with her pretty oval face tilted back and the yellow-beaded braids she used to wear swinging around her face. Bryan could almost remember the joke he'd told her to get her to laugh after she'd pointedly refused to smile for the camera. "On principle," she'd said. He'd kept the picture by his bed because it reminded him of everything he loved about Nina—her beauty, her humor, and her sense of principle.

Did I really ever believe Nina had all those qualities? Bryan marveled. His feelings for her seemed so far away, like all the other things that had once mattered to him. He ran his finger along the cracked glass, smearing a red wash of blood over the image of Nina's face.

It's the same with Nina as with everything else,

Bryan reflected as he gazed at the bloodstained photograph. He'd had to get rid of all his stuff because he was too attached to it. His possessions were starting to possess him instead of the other way around. *Just like I got too attached to Nina. I cared about her too much, and she started to control me.* Tears of rage welled up in Bryan's eyes, and Nina's image blurred into a bloody red wash before him. *I trusted her—and she used me. How could I have been so stupid?*

But he wasn't going to fall for any more of her lies, wasn't going to be so easily manipulated. *It was because I cared about Nina that she was able to control me,* Bryan told himself. *But I'm going to take back control. Because Nina means nothing to me now. And she never will again.*

Bryan felt the anger rise so high in him that for a moment it was all that existed. Trembling, he gripped the picture frame tightly in both hands and raised it above his head. He could feel blood trickling down his arms.

"Never again," Bryan whispered aloud in the stillness of the wildly disarrayed room. Then he flung Nina's picture as hard as he could against the bare wall and watched the glass shatter into a thousand pieces.

Chapter Six

I wish I had my sunglasses with me, Nina thought as she shielded her eyes with her hand, trying to adjust to the golden late afternoon sunlight that slanted through the trees lining the psych lab. *I feel disoriented enough without being blinded by bright lights.* Stepping outside was always a little overwhelming after two hours of confinement in the dimly lit cubicles and the trip through the mazelike hallways.

Nina blinked several times rapidly. When she opened her eyes, she caught sight of Bryan a few yards ahead of her, racing down the front steps of the psych lab.

Instinctively Nina opened her mouth to call out to him, but she caught herself almost immediately. There was no point in humiliating herself by shouting across campus to someone who wasn't going to turn around.

A presence at her side made Nina aware that she was still standing in front of the doorway of the psych lab, blocking the exit. Nina turned and was slightly taken aback to see Kerri standing there, wearing the same glazed, unreadable expression that had been stamped on her face for the past few days.

Should I talk to her? Nina wondered. She stepped aside to let Kerri pass and started down the stairs. After Kerri's scene in the dining hall, Nina wasn't sure if it would be a good idea to approach her. But now that they'd fallen into step beside each other, it seemed weird not to acknowledge her presence.

"Kerri, hi," Nina said loudly as they walked down the steps.

Kerri looked up with alarm, as if she hadn't realized Nina was right next to her. Her pace slowed as she searched Nina's face briefly. Then Nina saw recognition light in her eyes. "Hi, Nina," Kerri said finally, in a voice that was almost a whisper.

Nina grasped for something to say as they reached the bottom of the stairs. "So where are you headed?" she asked brightly.

Kerri's face clouded, and her eyes narrowed into a guarded expression. "Home," she said hoarsely.

Nina felt struck dumb by Kerri's trancelike coldness. For lack of anything better to say, she announced, "I'm off to biology. We're going to be discussing baldness. Pretty exciting, huh?"

To Nina's surprise, the ghost of a smile touched Kerri's face.

"My dream is that they'll find a cure in our lifetime," Nina continued, encouraged. "Because supposedly, you know, baldness is actually more common among women than men. So I figure if my time comes, I want to have some options." She grinned tentatively at Kerri, and this time Kerri returned a real smile. Nina let out her breath; she hadn't realized she'd been holding it.

"I've heard that, but I've never actually known any bald women," Kerri said in a much more animated voice.

The main SVU quad was teeming with students headed to and from classes. Outside in the fresh air, surrounded by ordinary, carefree people, Nina began to feel like she'd been ridiculous to imagine any connection between her problems with Bryan and Kerri's problems with eating.

Nothing but a coincidence, Nina assured herself. *College students are in crisis all the time—I know I am. I don't know what made me think there was any reason for those things happening at once.*

"My aunt Eunice was bald, but she always wore this huge bouffant wig," Nina noted. "One of the highlights of my childhood was the day I dared my cousin Jeffrey to steal it off her head at the church picnic."

"Oh no. The poor woman." Kerri laughed, her gray eyes crinkling warmly. Her expression was as open and friendly as on the day Nina had met her.

Maybe she's getting some help for her eating problem, Nina speculated. *What I saw must have been her hitting rock bottom.*

"Although I'm sure you got what was coming to you," Kerri remarked, still giggling.

"You bet. I think I'm actually still grounded, technically." Nina started to laugh as well, both at the memory and at her relief that Kerri seemed back to normal.

Behind Kerri, Nina saw a few guys in football uniforms approaching, obviously on their way back from practice. In front was a burly, tall, towheaded guy with a crew cut whom Nina recognized from a couple of frat parties Elizabeth and Jessica had dragged her to. His name was Brett or Biff or something. From what Nina had seen of him, which had mostly been in the vicinity of kegs, he was a loudmouth who enjoyed calling attention to his heterosexuality at every opportune moment.

Nina stopped laughing and cringed. Brett or Biff was obviously checking out Kerri from the rear and looked unpleasantly like he was about to make one of his little witty remarks.

"Hey, baby's got *back!*" Brett or Biff announced, guffawing loudly. His buddies, a beet-red-faced, heavyset, sandy-haired guy and a tall African American, chorused low, snorting laughter. The sandy-haired guy clapped his fearless leader on his padded shoulder. He was less than a foot away from Kerri now, and for a second Nina was afraid he was going to grab her.

Suddenly Kerri froze in her tracks. Nina saw that every trace of laughter was gone from her wide, terrified gray eyes.

Without turning around, without even appearing to move or breathe, Kerri reached behind her and seized Brett or Biff's wrist. He let out a little high-pitched yelp as she yanked hard on his arm. Before Nina had time to react, there was a wild blur of limbs . . . and then the football player was lying on his back on the ground. *Did she just flip him over with one hand?* Nina gaped, disbelieving.

Kerri's fists were clenched, and she was kicking frantically at the guy's torso as he feebly fought to push her away with his hands. "I won't let you get me!" she screeched through clenched teeth.

His friends, having recovered from their shock, moved in on Kerri to restrain her. "Hey, get off him, you psycho!" the blond guy yelled, reaching out toward one of Kerri's flailing arms.

But Kerri threw herself onto the guy on the ground and kept on hitting and scratching him in a frenzy. He shielded his face with his arms, but her hail of punches kept him from getting up. "You won't get me!" she screamed. "You're all after me, but I won't let you! I'll die first!"

As the guy's two buddies bent to wrestle Kerri off him the blond guy glanced up at Nina. "Hey, why don't you do something?" he shouted at her. "Are you as psycho as your friend? Can't you talk her down?"

"I—I don't know," Nina stammered, putting up her hands helplessly. "I don't know what's wrong with her." She knew they were expecting her to join in restraining Kerri, but Nina felt as if she were paralyzed. The sight of Kerri in a blind, violent frenzy, attacking another human being like a bloodthirsty animal, chilled Nina to the bone. *This can't be happening,* she thought frantically.

It took almost a minute for the two other guys to grab hold of Kerri and pull her off their friend. They dragged her to her feet. "Get a grip, you freak!" the African American guy cried, sounding deeply rattled.

Her arms restrained, Kerri whipped her head back and forth, still screeching. When she turned toward Nina, her round eyes had glazed over with terror and rage. Her pretty features were contorted into a mask of anguished dementia.

"You," she hissed in a strangled voice. "You planned this! You sent them to get me."

Nina backed slowly away, trembling. "No, Kerri, please, calm down. I didn't—"

"You did this!" Kerri screeched, in a voice so loud and inhuman that the football players shrank back slightly. Taking split-second advantage of their alarm, Kerri wrenched her arms free and took off running away from Nina.

As her figure receded into the distance, leaving a trail of openmouthed passersby, Nina could still hear Kerri shrieking: "I won't let you get me! You'll never catch me!"

Nina stood frozen in place, staring after Kerri, dimly aware of the football players helping their friend to his feet. She felt as if she were in a dream, where everything happening around her was absurd and random but had some elusive, underlying meaning.

She didn't know why Kerri had panicked like that, or why Bryan wasn't speaking to her, or why a perfectly normal young man her age had scratched himself raw. But now she was sure of one thing: It all had to do with the experiment.

The plump, middle-aged woman behind the snack bar gave Elizabeth her friendly, dimpled smile. "Not another salad?" she asked sympathetically.

Elizabeth looked up from the shelf of clear plastic containers she'd been inspecting, searching for the salad with the least-wilted spinach leaves. "Afraid so," she said, returning the smile. "I must have watched too many *Popeye* cartoons when I was little. I'm convinced that eating spinach is the only way I'll have enough energy to stay awake through my history reading."

The woman laughed. "Strong to the finish, right? Well, good luck. But you'd better have something a little more filling with it, or you'll be too hungry to concentrate."

"You're absolutely right," Elizabeth agreed, putting a bagel and a small plastic cup of cream cheese on her tray next to the spinach salad. "Well, I'm going to get this to go and eat in my room. I hope you have a nice night."

"You too, dear. Bye now," the woman said with a little wave. Elizabeth turned and headed toward the cash register, a faint smile still on her lips. *It sounds corny, but it does brighten your day to have those little friendly exchanges with people,* she reflected as the attendant rang up her food. A few minutes ago she'd been tense and stressed out after a marathon editing session at the WSVU station. On her way to the snack bar she'd obsessed about all the work she had ahead of her, deciding that after a quick dinner in her room she'd head straight to the library. Elizabeth still wasn't looking forward to the evening, but her spirits were slightly lifted by the sight of a friendly and familiar face. Even if it was somebody who knew her only as the girl who always got salads.

Elizabeth held out her hand as the cashier counted out her change. Then she waited as he put her food into a paper bag. The cashier was just reaching over the counter to hand Elizabeth her dinner, and she was opening her mouth to wish him a nice evening . . . when from the other end of the room there was a shrill, blood-curdling scream.

Elizabeth and the cashier both whirled around, and Elizabeth heard her bag of food fall to the floor. Across the room the plump face of the friendly snack bar woman was pale with terror. A gaunt young man with a dark, stringy ponytail had one arm around her neck and—Elizabeth realized with horror—was holding a knife to her throat. A ripple of noise and movement went through the crowd of students in the snack bar. The middle-aged woman who just moments ago had been smiling and joking with Elizabeth began to sob with fear.

"Shut up! Just shut up, all of you!" the young man shouted in a quivering voice. He cocked his head to one side, darting his eyes around the room. Elizabeth saw his hollow eyes widen as he surveyed the crowd staring at him—as if he were even more afraid than his hostage. "Nobody move! Nobody come near me, or I'll kill her!"

A girl somewhere behind Elizabeth screamed.

The cashier clutched the counter, looking as if he might faint. Elizabeth stood rooted where she was, unable to breathe. All she could think was, *I can't believe this is happening.* The guy looked as if he could have been an SVU student, with his long hair and goatee—he almost seemed eerily familiar, like someone Elizabeth had seen around campus. But his eyes were wild, haunted, like a deranged person's. She would have remembered someone like that.

"Everyone freeze—I said *freeze!*" the long-haired guy shrieked, brandishing his knife while holding the petrified woman headlocked in the crook of his other arm. "You're not going to get me—I want you all down on the ground!"

With fumbling slowness the students in the snack bar began lowering themselves onto the floor. Elizabeth lay on her stomach, acutely aware of the hammering of her heart against the tile. She prayed that nobody would panic and do anything that ended up getting that poor woman killed.

How could this be happening? Elizabeth wondered again. *Could this guy be on drugs?* If so, the problem on campus must be much worse than she had ever dreamed.

"You'd like that, wouldn't you?" the long-haired man went on, his voice high with hysteria. It was hard for Elizabeth to tell who he was talking to—the sobbing woman, the students cowering on the ground, or some imaginary audience of enemies. "You'd like to see me out of the way. But I won't let you get me! You won't get me!"

Elizabeth lifted her head in what she hoped was an imperceptibly small movement so she could get a good look at what was going on. To her horror, the guy was now grasping the worker by her uniform collar; the older woman's head was yanked back, her throat exposed. In his other hand he held the knife—a large butcher's knife, Elizabeth saw, that he must have snatched from behind the counter—over his head, poised as if to strike. The knife blade, reflecting the harsh neon lights of the cafeteria, glittered in the insane man's trembling hand.

His eyes flitted nervously across the room, as if he were looking for any sign of danger. As he glanced in Elizabeth's direction she quickly ducked her head down toward the floor . . . a split second too late. For a second she thought his glazed eyes were staring past her, out into space. But then they locked on hers.

"Keep your head down!" he raged as Elizabeth, terrified, pressed her cheek to the cool floor. "I'm not kidding around here. Don't make me shed any blood!"

Elizabeth's whole body was trembling even as she willed herself to lie as still as possible. *What have I done?* she berated herself. *Now I could be his next target!* She wished desperately that she hadn't called attention to herself.

"Do I have to shed blood? *Do I?*" the young man cried. Elizabeth could feel his eyes on her, but she didn't dare look up. "Because I will!"

He's really going to kill her, Elizabeth realized, stricken. *And if I make a wrong move, he might kill me.* Silent tears of anger, fear, and helplessness began to spill from her eyes as suddenly and violently as the scene before her had unrolled. *I don't want to die like this. It's so unfair! How could someone snap like that here at SVU?* Elizabeth had no idea what kind of recreational drug made a person so inhumanly . . . what? Cruel? Paranoid? Delusional?

Just inhuman, Elizabeth decided, biting her lip to keep from sobbing aloud. If she made any noise, he'd kill her for sure.

"Please, mister," the woman whispered, her pitiful voice filling the room like a siren.

"Freeze! We've got you covered!" an unfamiliar male voice barked suddenly.

Startled, Elizabeth dared to lift her head and saw a blue blur of movement behind the crazed young man. *Of course! The security cameras!* she thought with relief as campus security guards surrounded the guy. She sent out a silent prayer that they would be able to restrain him without getting his hostage killed in the process.

112

In a flash the whole room was in motion. As the guards closed in on the wild-eyed man—who began screeching steadily as soon as he saw them—students started getting to their feet, running for the nearest exits. Several were screaming or, like Elizabeth, had tears streaming down their faces.

Elizabeth had to scramble to her feet to avoid being trampled by the rush of panicked people. But she couldn't bring herself to leave until she saw that the woman was safe. She flattened herself against the counter and craned her head to see over the crowd. To her immense relief, she saw that the middle-aged woman was safely in the arms of a security guard.

But the long-haired guy was still struggling with four or five guards, two of whom were engaged in trying to pry the knife from his hands. Elizabeth caught her breath as the knife veered dangerously close to one guard's face. "You'll never get me! You'll never take me alive!" the deranged man still grunted as he fought for control of the weapon.

Finally the security guards, along with a few policemen who had arrived amid the commotion, overwhelmed the young man and managed to handcuff his hands behind his back. Elizabeth felt weak in her knees with relief. *Everything is going to be all right,* she told herself.

113

As the police led the guy through the thinning crowd he continued to rant—as if he had no idea where he was, no idea that a moment ago he'd been in control and now was in captivity. "You can't get me . . . I won't let you. . . ."

Even though the attacker was safely in police custody, Elizabeth felt a cold shiver of fear run down her spine. Now that the ordeal was over, her mind had made a troubling connection. The way that guy had been ranting . . . it reminded Elizabeth of the druggie she'd seen the other day. Not that she thought they were the same person—the first guy had had short hair and been clean shaven. But there was something similar about their ravings.

As if they were on the same drug or had the same . . . whatever the problem is, Elizabeth thought. Somehow drugs didn't seem like an adequate explanation, but Elizabeth couldn't come up with a better one.

People don't just all of a sudden go crazy, Elizabeth argued to herself as she headed out of the snack bar, her appetite totally forgotten. *And definitely not at the same time, like it was catching.* It didn't add up. As difficult as it was to believe, maybe the coinciding events were just that—a coincidence.

Nina jumped when the phone on her desk rang. She waited another ring so the pounding of

114

her heart could slow before picking up the receiver. "Hello?"

"Hi, Nina, it's me." Elizabeth's voice sounded somehow meeker than usual. "Are you—do you have a minute?"

"Sure, Liz, what's up? Are you OK?" Nina got up, taking the phone with her, and sat down at the foot of her bed. Elizabeth's ominous tone was doing nothing to quench the acid adrenaline rush Nina had gotten when she was startled by the phone.

"Well," Elizabeth said shakily, "I am now, but this really insane thing happened to me. Well, not exactly to me, but . . ." Nina heard Elizabeth inhale deeply. "I was in the snack bar when this guy totally freaked out. I mean really snapped."

Nina had a terrible sinking feeling. "Snapped?" she echoed hoarsely.

"Uh-huh. He pulled a knife on this poor woman and made everybody get down on the floor." Elizabeth paused to take another deep breath. "Security got everything under control after a few minutes, but it was just so weird, Nina. I mean, the guy looked like a student. Doesn't it seem crazy that an SVU student would do something like that?"

Nina gripped the phone tightly and closed her eyes. "What did he look like?"

"Um . . . he had long brown hair in a ponytail.

And a goatee. I think he had a leather jacket on. Why?"

Nina was silent. *The guy with the ponytail and goatee had a leather jacket on today,* she recalled, thinking back to the experiment session.

"Nina?"

Nina shook herself back to the present. "Sorry, Liz. I was just . . . like you said, it's pretty heavy that that happened here on campus. I was just kind of digesting it."

Nina hesitated. It was tempting to share her suspicions with Elizabeth—at the start of the year they'd built their friendship on confiding in each other when neither of them felt she had anyone else to turn to. Usually Nina wouldn't have thought twice about whether Elizabeth would think less of her if Nina shared a secret. *But this isn't like guy trouble or being stressed about tests. This is . . . I don't even know* what *this is,* Nina realized grimly. *For all I know, it's my imagination. If I tell Elizabeth I think this craziness goes back to the experiment, she'll think* I'm *the one who's lost my mind. And I'm not sure I could argue with her there.*

"Listen," Nina went on. "That's a pretty scary thing to have happen to you. If you want, I'll come over later and we can just hang out or study. I'm sure you don't feel like being alone." *If I can't tell Liz my secret, I can at least offer her some support, Nina thought with a fresh twinge of guilt.*

"That would be great, Nina." Elizabeth sounded relieved. "But I actually feel like I need to lie down for a while and chill out. Maybe take a nap. Do you think you could stop by in a couple of hours and bang on my door? If I'm not up by then, I'll definitely wake up when you knock."

"This dorm doesn't exactly have the thickest walls in the world," Nina agreed. "These doors are what, plywood?"

"I think they expect students to lock themselves out of their rooms and have to break down the doors all the time," Elizabeth speculated, sounding closer to her normal cheerful self. "That must be why they don't think it's worth investing in sturdy building materials. I mean, it *couldn't* be that the SVU housing department doesn't care about us."

Nina laughed. Elizabeth was definitely recovering. "Of course not. OK, Liz, sweet dreams. I'll see you in a couple of hours."

Chapter Seven

I'm glad I managed to cheer Liz up, Nina reflected as she hung up the phone, *but it was only because I didn't tell her my secret.* She closed her eyes and dropped her face into her hands. *Elizabeth always reminds me I can tell her anything,* Nina thought guiltily. *I feel horrible not being totally honest with her.*

But what would I have said to her? Nina argued with herself. She had no idea what was going on, except that the experiment seemed somehow to be changing people. Almost . . . driving them crazy. And the worst part of it was that her whole theory was so far-fetched, she kept wondering if *she* was the one going crazy. She couldn't help worrying that if she shared her bizarre-sounding suspicions with Elizabeth, Elizabeth would believe . . . that she needed professional help.

Nina groaned. It was like a paradox: If the experiment made people go insane, it seemed impossible that she would remain unaffected to realize it. But if she was just being paranoid and imagining strange occurrences where there were none, that seemed to prove her theory that the experiment was causing people to become delusional.

But how? And why? Is it happening for a reason, or is it just some weird side effect? Nina's head swam with questions that she barely even understood how to pose, let alone answer.

Who would want to do this to students? She thought back to the cold, standoffish Dr. Akre. *Could he possibly* intend *for all these terrible things to happen?* The guy was weird, but that didn't mean he was *evil*.

Nina groaned aloud and jerked her head upright. *Nothing makes sense,* she thought miserably. She just kept turning confused thoughts over and over in her mind while around her people were changing, losing touch with reality.

Like Bryan. Nina bit her lip. *The fact that our relationship is completely nonexistent is bad enough.* But if Bryan were to do something as awful as the things she and Elizabeth had seen . . . if he actually *attacked* someone . . . The idea was more than Nina could bear.

Nina still hoped against hope that things would work out between her and Bryan—maybe when and if she figured out what was going on with the experiment—but she wasn't a glutton for punishment. A human being could only be shot down by the person they loved so many times before it became too painful to try anymore.

But now I know something definite, Nina realized with a sinking feeling in the pit of her stomach. *Well, not definite exactly, but I know that the experiment is not what it seems to be.* And now that she knew that, she owed it to Bryan to try one more time to get through to him. *I owe it to both of us. To our relationship.*

Nina's sinking feeling had grown so strong that she felt as if the pit of her stomach were bottomless. But she had to make sure that Bryan didn't end up like those others. That he didn't try to hurt anybody.

She tried to convince herself that persuading Bryan to see reason would be no big deal. *Maybe it'll be like one of those revelations people have at the end of TV shows. Where somebody tells them how badly they've been treating other people, and they apologize and never do it again.*

But even the thought of TV made Nina think of being strapped into that chair, watching those ads. And remembering what that felt like, there was no way Nina could pretend this was going to be easy.

Exhaling deeply, Nina picked up the phone on her desk and cocked her head to hold it in place.

As she dialed Bryan's number Nina scratched the back of her neck with her free hand. *Just thinking about the experiment makes me uncomfortable and itchy,* she realized as she listened to the phone ring on the other end of the line.

After four or five more rings, just as Nina was getting ready to hang up, an unfamiliar, flat voice answered the phone. "Hello."

"Hello . . . could I speak to Bryan, please?" Nina responded. *Did I dial a wrong number?* she wondered, puzzled.

There was a pause on the other end of the line. Then the voice, clipped and defensive, said, "This *is* Bryan. Who is this?" Nina gulped. It was unthinkable that Bryan could have changed so much that she couldn't even recognize his voice—the voice that had whispered "I love you" a thousand times, that had comforted and encouraged her when she was down.

But obviously the unthinkable had happened. Nina would never have recognized that cold, dead voice as Bryan's.

"This is Nina," she managed finally. "Bryan, I need to talk to you. Please don't hang up—just listen for a minute."

Another pause. "I'm listening," the frozen voice said.

"Well," Nina plunged ahead bravely, "it's about the experiment."

"The experiment," Bryan echoed hollowly. Nina wasn't sure if there really was a mocking note in his voice or if she'd imagined it.

"Yeah, the experiment. Listen, Bryan. Some of the people who are in the experiment with us—a *lot* of them, actually—are acting really weird. I think there's something going on. Something we're not being told."

Silence.

Nina swallowed hard. She had to get it all out. "Bryan, I think that all the problems we've had . . . all your anger at me . . . I don't think it's about me, Bryan. I think it's somehow related to the experiment. I don't know why yet, but the experiment is *making* people react really violently to completely normal things. I think if you would just give me a chance, we could figure out what's going on. What it is they're not telling us, Dr. Akre or—whatever that company is that he's working for. And we could save our relationship. Please, Bryan, I don't want to give up on you. I love you more than anything."

Nina held her breath. There was a long, charged silence on the other end of the line. Once Nina thought she heard a sharp intake of breath, as if Bryan had been about to say something but then bitten it back. *Is he wrestling with himself?* Nina wondered. For an instant she dared to hope that Bryan might be coming around. Was it possible her words had gotten through to him?

Then, after a minute that seemed to Nina like an eternity, Bryan spoke again.

"What they're not telling us, huh," Bryan said coldly. His rich, deep voice—which had given so many thundering speeches at BSU conventions, which had whispered countless sweet nothings that sent shivers through Nina's whole body— was flattened out into an even, uninflected line. "How about what *you're* not telling *me*? Come on, Nina, did you really expect me to believe all those lies? How stupid do you think I am?" Bryan spat out the word *stupid* as if throwing it back in Nina's face.

He paused for breath, and when he continued, his voice trembled with suppressed rage. "I can't believe you would make up a pack of lies like that just to try to deflect the blame from yourself."

"Bryan, please, I know it sounds crazy, but . . ." Nina cried out in spite of herself. It was obvious that anything she said would just infuriate Bryan more, but it was too painful to hear him talk like that. Hot tears sprang to Nina's eyes.

"Save your breath. I see what you're doing, Nina," Bryan charged, the fury in his voice mounting. "Oh, so I'm not really angry at you, am I? So it's not about you? Well, I hate to burst your bubble, but I'm not the gullible guy I once was. This *is* about you—you trying to manipulate me. I'm not just going to come crawling back to you because you tell me I can trust you. I know you're just making up all these stories about the experiment to make me *think* I can trust you. So you'll have me under your thumb again like you used to."

"Bryan, no . . . ," Nina whispered through her tears. But she was too overcome to continue. She broke down and wept into the mouthpiece of the phone, clutching the receiver like it was the last thread that connected her to Bryan—to the way her life used to be.

"Spare me the waterworks." Bryan's icy voice cut through Nina like a knife. "I'm over it. I'm over you trying to manipulate me, to use me for whatever you want. I know the only reason you're pretending to care about me is so you can control me. *Destroy me.* And I'm not going to let you."

"Destroy? What—" Nina choked helplessly through her sobs. "Bryan, listen to what you're saying. . . ."

"I won't let you," Bryan repeated, his voice cracking slightly. "You're not going to get to me. Good-bye, Nina. It was fun while I was deluded. But now it's over. I'm cutting you out of my life."

There was a forceful clattering noise on the other end of the line, as if Bryan had slammed down the receiver so hard that it bounced off its cradle. Then the line went dead. For a moment there was silence; then a recorded voice came on. *"There appears to be a receiver off the hook. Please hang up and try your call again."*

Nina just sat frozen where she was, still gripping the phone, almost as if she thought Bryan would come back on the line and take back everything he had just said. She was too stunned to move. She couldn't breathe for the ache in her chest. Never in a million years would she have expected her relationship with Bryan to end like this. The Bryan she'd known and loved just a matter of days ago had never been so harsh, so brutally hurtful. He'd never shut her out like that.

Nina slowly lowered the receiver onto its cradle. *The person I just talked to wasn't Bryan,* she realized. The experiment had changed him somehow, changed him beyond recognition. The question was, would she ever see the real Bryan again? Or had she tried too late to reach him?

Nina wasn't sure. In fact, she'd never felt so unsure of anything in her whole life.

Nina put down her pen and reached for the roll of toilet paper on her desk. She'd snagged it from the bathroom down the hall about an hour ago, when she'd run out of Kleenex, and since then she'd managed to go through about half the roll. Nina unrolled several squares and tore them off. She dabbed at her blotchy, swollen cheekbones, wiping away the latest round of tears.

It had been over two hours since she'd talked to Bryan, and she still hadn't stopped crying. Nina hadn't cried this much since her grandmother died four years ago. She didn't think she had ever felt so confused and alone.

She blew her nose into the toilet paper, then wadded it up and tossed it into her already overflowing wastebasket. Then, turning her attention back to the open journal before her on the desk, Nina picked up her pen again. *It's just so hard to sort out all my feelings,* she wrote. *I know that whatever is wrong with Bryan has to do with the experiment. It's not about me. But it still hurts so much.* A fresh round of tears sprang to Nina's eyes. One dropped onto the journal, blurring a little cloud of words. *And I don't know if I'm strong enough to go after the truth about the experiment with Bryan not on my side. More than not on my side—actively against me.* Nina underlined the word *against* heavily. As the page swam before her eyes she put down her pen and reached for the roll of toilet paper again.

When she'd wiped the tears away and blown her stuffed-up nose, Nina suddenly smelled something in the air. *That girl down the hall must be smoking in her room again,* she thought with annoyance. *She's lucky I don't call the RA and get her busted.* Nina hated smoking, but she wasn't a snitch. Besides, she had way too much on her mind to get stressed out by petty dorm disputes. She picked up her pen again.

Just then an obnoxious clanging noise filled the air. Startled, Nina dropped her pen.

"The fire alarm!" she exclaimed aloud. "Didn't we just have a drill last week?"

As the alarm continued to sound insistently, drowning out everything else from Nina's consciousness, she reluctantly got up and went to the door. *Great, just what I needed,* she thought sarcastically. *Now everybody in Dickenson Hall can see me crying like an idiot.*

Nina reached out to grasp the doorknob. It was warm, and she drew back her hand. Then she looked down and saw smoke seeping into the room from underneath the door.

Her heart began to pound. "This isn't a fire drill," she muttered. "This is real! The dorm is on fire! I—I have to get out of here!"

Quickly Nina grabbed the tan wool cardigan that was draped over the back of her desk chair. Using the wadded-up sweater to protect her hands from the heat, she turned the doorknob and flung open the door. Instantly Nina was surrounded by smoke. Coughing violently, she waved her arms in front of her face in a vain attempt to clear the air.

A couple of students appeared briefly from

deep within the wall of smoke and ran screaming past Nina, headed toward the fire exit. They hadn't gone more than a few feet past her before they disappeared again into the smoke. Nina stumbled forward, still coughing, following in the direction they'd gone. Her eyes, already sore from crying, stung in the thick smoke. Her chest was still racked with sobs, now more from panic than grief, and it was almost impossible to breathe. *If I can just make it to fresh air, I'll be fine,* Nina told herself.

She felt her way along the wall toward the fire exit. More students ran past her, almost knocking her to the side. Nina could hear screams and voices calling out to one another, though she couldn't see anyone. In the distance behind her, over the incessant shrill of the fire alarm, she heard someone pounding on doors and a deep male voice shouting for everyone to come out.

Elizabeth! Nina suddenly realized. She'd said she was going to take a nap. *What if she doesn't hear them knocking on her door?* Nina's heart thudded violently against her rib cage. *I couldn't live with myself if anything happened to Liz. I have to go make sure she's OK.*

Nina turned around, about to head down the hall the way she'd come, but almost collided with a tall, broad-chested firefighter. Nina looked up at his soot-smeared face in surprise.

"Miss, I'm afraid I can't let you go back there. Just keep moving toward the exit," the firefighter boomed over the wailing of the alarm, putting a hand on Nina's shoulder to steer her back around.

"But my friend," Nina protested hysterically, trying to shrug herself out of his grip. "She's asleep in her room. I have to make sure she's safe!"

The firefighter grasped Nina's arm firmly and pushed her toward the exit. "We have everything under control, miss. Firefighters are on the job. We can't have people running all over the building. You must evacuate. Your friend will be fine."

Her heart sinking, Nina was pushed down the hall in another tide of shrieking dormmates. *I hope he's right,* she thought fearfully as she hurried toward the fire exit. *For Elizabeth's sake.*

So hot in here, Elizabeth thought. *Why is it so hot?* She was back in the snack bar, flattened against the floor while the deranged young man with the ponytail ranted and threatened his hostage. But when she pressed her cheek to the tile floor, it felt hot, not cool, to her touch.

And all the students were screaming. *Why are they screaming so loudly?* Elizabeth thought, panic rising in her throat. *They're going to get us all killed.* She glanced around at the students writhing uncontrollably on the floor, howling. *Why won't they stay still? We're all going to die!*

129

"Keep quiet!" Elizabeth yelled aloud.

But the noise in the room just got louder as one shrill, insistent note rose over all the screams, filling the room. "Quiet!" Elizabeth moaned, thrashing on the floor. The room began to fill with smoke. She couldn't breathe. She looked down at the floor beneath her face and saw that it was covered with blood. . . .

Elizabeth woke up with a start to find that she really *was* surrounded by smoke. The fire alarm was blaring, and she could hear screams from the hallway.

"Jess?" Elizabeth called out blurrily, disoriented from her nap and from the smoke. Then she shook herself to consciousness and remembered Jessica wasn't there. She was alone in the smoke-filled room.

A split second later the full realization that she was trapped in a burning building dawned on her. Elizabeth bolted upright from the bed. Throwing back the covers, she jumped out of her sweat-soaked bedclothes and slipped her feet into the black Converse sneakers by her bed. Heading for the door, she thanked her lucky stars that she'd been too shaken when she got home to change out of her T-shirt and jeans before burrowing under her covers.

When she touched the door, it felt hot. Elizabeth grabbed a towel off the floor of Jessica's side of the room and used it to turn the doorknob.

As she opened the door a wave of smoke hit her. Coughing, she shielded her face with her hand. For a moment the smoke thinned. Down the hall, from the student lounge by the stairwell, tongues of flame darted out to lick the walls of the narrow corridor. As Elizabeth hovered fearfully in the doorway of room 28 the flames stretched closer toward her.

"That's the way to the fire exit!" Elizabeth cried. "How am I going to get out?"

Chapter Eight

"Burn! Burn it clean!" Bryan whispered. He inhaled deeply, drinking in the heady scent of the smoke. It was such blessed relief, such joy, to see the building smolder. To watch as the soothing fingers of flame burned everything clean. In the distance the cacophony of sirens and screams was like sweet music to his ears.

"Fire! Fire! Fire!" Bryan chanted softly to himself, his fists clenched. "Burn away the filth! Burn away the evil!"

He stepped out from behind the tree so he could get a better look at the blaze. Flames leaped from one window that glowed red like a knowing eye, winking at Bryan. Thick gray smoke poured from the other windows on the floor. Although he didn't quite know why, just the sight of the burning building made him feel better; the tight knot of rage lodged in his chest had loosened and lifted off him as gently as the smoke drifting out of the windows and across the sky.

Bryan smiled blissfully with the knowledge that the fire would cleanse the building, stripping everybody inside of all the things they didn't need, all the useless trappings that weighed them down. Just like he'd purged his own life of his belongings, of his so-called friends. *Of Nina,* Bryan thought, wincing at the mental echo of her name. It was like a dirty word to him now.

Bryan forced himself to focus on the rising fingers of flame before the thought of Nina made the knot in his chest clench up again. The fire was beautiful, graceful. So much more beautiful than the twisted, flailing bodies of students that were swarming out of the smoky entrance like insects from a hive.

Suddenly Bryan saw a familiar figure emerge from the crowd of students pouring out of the building. She was coming toward him, looking right at him. Bryan felt the anger fill his chest, choking him. It was as if Nina were some kind of demon, and by thinking of her, he had invoked her.

"Bryan!" Nina called in a desperate voice. As she came closer Bryan could see that her face was swollen, as if she'd been crying. Fear and confusion filled her eyes.

Bryan retreated behind the tree and pressed

his forehead against the trunk, trying to clear his mind of the wave of red rage that had overcome him. He felt as if *he* were on fire instead of the building. *That's where Nina lives,* he realized, trembling with an overwhelming mixture of conflicting emotions.

Bryan knew he was glad to be free of Nina. He'd been overcome with joy to watch her home burn. But seeing her now, looking so helpless and lost . . . it made his heart ache with something other than anger. Something that felt like the ghost of a feeling he'd had a long time ago, perhaps in a dream.

"Bryan!" Nina called out again. Soon she would be close enough for him to reach out and touch her. *I have to get out of here,* Bryan realized in a panic. He wasn't sure whether being near Nina would force him to hurt her or tempt him to fall under her evil spell again. And he was terrified of finding out.

Bryan spun on his heel and ran as fast as he could across the darkened campus. He was dimly aware of Nina still calling his name in the distance. But her voice was soon swallowed up by the sounds of the commotion around them.

"Don't worry, we're going to get you out of here."

Elizabeth turned, startled, toward the friendly

voice she heard at her elbow. A tall firefighter stood holding a fire extinguisher. "Just follow me, OK?"

Elizabeth nodded, smiling gratefully. She was still nervous, but she fell into step behind the firefighter. As they made their way down the hall he let loose a few blasts with the fire extinguisher to clear their path. "You all right back there?" he asked with a slight turn of his head.

"Fine," Elizabeth called out with more confidence than she felt. "I think."

As they approached the student lounge on the corner of the hall Elizabeth could see that the flames appeared to be coming from the lounge. *We have to walk by there to get to the stairwell!* Elizabeth realized with trepidation. *Can we really get past safely?*

Suddenly there was a loud cracking noise from above their heads, and a shower of plaster rained down all around them. With frightening speed a fiery beam fell from the ceiling and landed in front of the firefighter, missing him by a fraction of an inch. Elizabeth screamed.

"It's OK, miss, you're going to be all right." The firefighter stopped, turned, and hefted Elizabeth over his shoulder as if she were a sack of potatoes. Swiftly he raced past the burning beam, angling his body so that Elizabeth was shielded from the flames.

As they passed the student lounge Elizabeth

peered through the shattered glass windows that lined the room. It was hard to see clearly through the smoke, but she could make out two figures struggling in the flames. Over the wail of the fire alarm Elizabeth heard a shrill, high-pitched voice cry, "Burn, fire! Let it burn! Burn away the evil! Burn it all clean!"

As the smoke shifted, Elizabeth could see that one of the figures wore a firefighter's helmet and appeared to be grappling with a smaller person— a young woman she didn't recognize—who was flailing and kicking wildly.

"Let me stay!" the girl shrieked between hacking, smoke-filled coughs as the firefighter fought to pull her toward the hallway. "I have to stay and watch it burn. . . . I have to see the evil burn away!"

Despite the sweltering heat of the fiery hall, Elizabeth felt a chill run up her spine. *She sounds so crazed, just like that guy in the snack bar . . . and the druggie by the math building,* she realized. *I can't believe she's strong enough to resist that firefighter!*

"Burn it away—don't let it touch me! Burn the evil clean, burn it clean!" the voice shrilled. Elizabeth caught one last glimpse of pale arms writhing in smoky air before the dark billows of smoke swallowed up the figures.

She'd been so focused on escaping the burning

building that she hadn't given any thought to how the fire had started. But now Elizabeth realized with horror that it was that girl who must have started it . . . on purpose. *If you can call pyromania a purpose,* Elizabeth thought.

They had reached the stairwell, and the firefighter was setting her on her feet. "You think you'll be OK to head out by yourself? I'm going to go back and see if that other firefighter needs some help getting that young lady to safety."

Elizabeth nodded. "I'm fine. Good luck—and thanks for saving my life."

The firefighter grinned. "All in a day's work," he said lightly. But as he turned away and headed back out into the hall, Elizabeth thought she saw his shoulders slump. *No wonder he's worried,* she thought. *If that girl doesn't want to be rescued, he and that other firefighter could get trapped in that lounge with her.*

The idea was too horrible to think about. Elizabeth wound her way down the stairwell, breathing the clearer air in deeply. She still couldn't really believe all this was happening—maybe she hadn't really woken up from her nightmare.

All these strange things happening at once, Elizabeth mused as she caught up with several other students who were filing down the stairs. SVU was a large university, but several students having mental breakdowns in the space of a few days was statistically about as likely as an alien spacecraft landing on campus. All Elizabeth's instincts told her that something terrifyingly wrong was happening at SVU. But she couldn't for the life of her imagine what.

There's something Nina's not telling me—something that's really putting her on edge, Elizabeth reflected as she reached the bottom of the stairs. *So what is she hiding? Does it have anything to do with these insane incidents?*

Nina hadn't thought she had any tears left, but when she saw Elizabeth stumble out of the building looking as if she'd just rolled out of bed, Nina's eyes immediately grew moist with relief. She'd never been so happy to see her friend. "Elizabeth! You're safe!" Her arms outstretched, she ran toward her friend.

Elizabeth returned Nina's embrace warmly. "Yeah, I'm OK, Nina. How about you?"

"I've been better," Nina admitted as they pulled apart, their arms still around each other's shoulders. "But at least I wasn't hurt in the fire. I was mostly worried about you."

"I'm fine. A firefighter helped me get out of my room." Elizabeth stared up at the burning dormitory. "I just hope our stuff isn't totally destroyed. I don't know what Jessica would do if she came home to find that all her clothes had been burned to a crisp."

"I don't know what I'm going to do if all my stuff's gone either," Nina said with a sigh. "I'm not earning *that* much at the experiment." She followed Elizabeth's gaze up to Dickenson. Firefighters were busy with hoses, trying to contain the blaze. It seemed to have died down somewhat, but small flames still leaped from one window. "How could this have happened anyway? Did someone drop a cigarette or something?"

Elizabeth seemed to hesitate for a moment. "I don't think it was an accident," she said finally.

Nina felt her blood run cold. She slipped her arm off Elizabeth's shoulders. "What do you mean?" she asked, trying to keep the feeling of dread out of her voice.

"The fire looked like it was coming from the second-floor lounge," Elizabeth began slowly. "When the firefighter carried me past, there was someone in there. She looked kind of like this girl who lives down the hall from me. But she was saying all this weird stuff, ranting like . . . like the guy in the snack bar today."

Like Bryan, Nina thought. *And Kerri too.*

"It was like she was happy about the fire," Elizabeth went on. "I'm pretty sure that she set it and that it *wasn't* an accident . . . at least not as far as she was concerned."

"She set the fire. . . ." Nina stared off into the distance. The smoke rising from Dickenson Hall clouded the dark, clear night, but behind the haze she could see the full moon glowing in a perfect circle.

Nina was tempted to ask Elizabeth for a description, but she knew she didn't need one. At this point she could no longer hide behind the possibility of coincidence. It had just been burned away.

"What is it, Nina?" Elizabeth furrowed her brow with concern and a touch of impatience.

After a moment Nina seemed to register that Elizabeth had asked her a question. She shook her head. "Nothing, Liz. I just can't believe someone would set fire to our dorm on purpose."

Elizabeth looked down at her shoes to hide her frustration. She had been through a lot today, and the last thing she needed was for her best friend to be keeping secrets from her. Nina obviously knew something, and Elizabeth was starting to worry about what exactly she knew . . . and how. *What if Nina's involved somehow?* Elizabeth thought for a panicked moment.

But that was impossible. Nina was her best friend, no matter how strangely she'd been acting lately.

This is crazy, Elizabeth decided. *I'm starting to imagine things. I have to confront her.*

"Nina, please tell me what's going on. Maybe it's something I can help with."

Nina hesitated for a fraction of a second.

"Nothing," she said quickly. "Nothing's going on. I . . . I don't know what you mean."

"But we *both* know that some bizarre things have been happening lately," Elizabeth persisted. "And the way you've been acting—"

"What do you mean, 'the way I've been acting'?" Nina demanded, cutting Elizabeth off. "I'm fine! Are you saying I've been acting weird? Don't, because I'm *fine*, OK, Liz?"

"Fine"—that's what Bryan said too, Elizabeth thought exhaustedly. *Not acting weird, huh? Well, whatever. I don't have the energy to push Nina right now.* They were both shaken up, their nerves frayed. There was no point in pressing Nina further about something she obviously didn't want to discuss—not after what they'd just been through anyway.

When my head is clearer, I'll figure out a way of bringing it up, Elizabeth resolved as she dug her hands into her pockets. After all, she was a reporter. She was generally very good at getting information out of people. But it wasn't every day that her life was in jeopardy more than once. One more stressful situation might send her over the deep end.

Elizabeth found what she was looking for in her pockets: the quarter she'd carried in case of emergencies ever since she was old enough to leave the house without her parents' supervision.

"Listen, I'll be right back," she announced to Nina, holding up the quarter. "I'm heading over to a pay phone to call Steven. I'm assuming Dickenson will be closed at least for tonight, so maybe I can crash there. The way I see it, older brothers exist to have their privacy invaded, especially when they live off campus."

Nina, still looking at the ground, didn't crack a smile. "Do you want me to see if it's cool for you to share the fold-out couch with me?" Elizabeth added gently.

"Thanks, Liz," Nina replied softly, still not meeting Elizabeth's eyes. "That would be great."

"Sure," Elizabeth said. "Don't go anywhere. I'll meet you back here in a minute."

She headed toward the student union building, suddenly feeling very glad to be calling her big brother. Steven and his girlfriend, Billie, were always there for her when she was stressed out about anything.

Nina's usually there for me too, Elizabeth conceded as she walked across campus, clutching her emergency quarter tightly in the palm of her hand. *But right now something's going on in her life that's more than she can handle. I just wish she would tell me what it is before anybody else gets hurt.*

Chapter Nine

Where is he? Nina turned and paced the length of the tiny cubicle for what felt like the hundredth time. It took her three steps before she turned again and walked back. *When is he going to get here?* she wondered, sighing with impatience. She felt like a caged animal, but she didn't want to sit in that chair and stare at that enormous glowing TV screen for one moment longer than she had to.

Besides, I want to be standing up when I confront Christian, Nina reminded herself. *I can't talk to him while he's hooking me up to all those wires like the bride of Frankenstein.*

The night before at Steven's, while Elizabeth slept peacefully beside her on the pullout couch, Nina had lain awake and asked herself countless questions for which she had no answers. She knew she had to do something about the experiment soon, before her fears drove her completely insane. But until she had some concrete facts to go on, Nina was helpless to take action. Christian seemed to be her most likely source of information.

Nina had no idea if the terrifying effects of the experiment were intentional, if they were real to begin with, or if Christian himself was aware of anything. But she had no doubt that getting in Dr. Akre's face with thinly veiled accusations would not be a smart move. *I don't think I've ever even talked to the guy about the weather, much less asked him if he's purposely driving SVU students insane,* Nina thought wryly. Christian would definitely be much easier to talk to.

Nina traversed the room a few more times before the door opened and Christian came in. He flashed her his friendly grin, exposing rows of perfect white teeth. He was wearing a light blue T-shirt under his lab coat that set off his cappuccino-colored skin perfectly. He was just as gorgeous as he had been the day Nina first saw him. But now his attractiveness seemed like something she had noticed in another existence, when unimportant things mattered to her. Before her life had been turned upside down.

"Hi, Nina. How's it going today?" Still smiling, Christian gestured for her to have a seat in the chair.

Nina made no effort to move from where she

stood at the back of the room. She stared across the chair at Christian, summoning her courage. "Actually I'm not doing so great."

Christian looked slightly taken aback. His grin faded. "Oh? Why's that?"

"Well, let's see," Nina began. "In the past couple of days my boyfriend broke up with me, my best friend was held hostage in the snack bar, and someone set my dorm on fire." She ticked the items off on her fingertips as she spoke. "Kind of a streak of bad luck, wouldn't you say?"

Christian's expression was guarded. "I'm sorry to hear that, Nina. But we should really get started—"

"I don't want to get started. I want some answers." Nina put her hands on her hips and took a deep breath. "Because Christian, you know what's even weirder?"

"What?" Christian's face remained expressionless, but his voice broke slightly.

"Every single student who's started acting strangely—my boyfriend, Bryan; the guy who held my friend hostage; the woman who started the fire—is one of the subjects of this experiment."

Christian folded his arms across his chest. "Nina, what are you trying to say?"

"I'm trying to say that the people involved in this experiment are changing." Nina searched Christian's impassive face intently. "People don't just randomly go insane in the space of a few

145

days. And I want to know why this is happening. There's something we're not being told." She looked expectantly at Christian.

To Nina's surprise, a dark scowl crossed his face. "Look, just because you have problems with your love life doesn't mean that everybody around you is going crazy," Christian snapped harshly. "Maybe you have some issues with projecting and displacing guilt. Not to mention paranoia."

Nina's jaw dropped open. "How dare you—"

"The health services building can refer you to some excellent therapists with sliding-scale fees for students," Christian continued, as if he hadn't heard her. "But I'm afraid I don't have time to work out your issues here. If you don't get hooked up, we can't start the session. So if you don't mind sitting down—"

"I *do* mind!" Nina shouted furiously. "You can't talk to me like that! This experiment is out of control, and I don't want to be a part of it anymore. I'm out of here." She stormed toward the door.

"Nina, this is ridiculous." Christian hovered in the doorway, blocking her exit. "This experiment is being conducted by Dr. Charles Akre, an honored member of the global scientific community. How could there be anything going on that wasn't completely ethical and aboveboard?"

"That's what I'm going to find out," Nina retorted. "Now, if you'll excuse me."

Christian stood aside to let her pass, and Nina

stormed out of the cubicle and down the deserted corridor. *I can't believe Christian put me down that harshly,* she fumed, tears of rage and frustration filling her eyes as she pushed open the door to the stairwell. *Talk about projecting guilt! The way he just freaked out on me only makes me more sure that something sinister is going on . . . and it's no accident.*

Unless, of course, she really *was* going crazy, just as Christian had said. His words echoed in her mind. *Displacement . . . paranoia . . .*

It's not like he tried very hard to convince me to stay, Nina realized. *Maybe he figured the experiment was better off without a loose cannon like me.*

"Could all this really be my imagination?" Nina wiped her tears on her sleeve. "Am I really losing my mind?" Bryan and Christian seemed to think so. And if Elizabeth hadn't thought Nina was going crazy before last night, Nina's defensive outburst had no doubt confirmed it in her mind.

The more she thought about it, it seemed far less likely that the whole world had turned upside down in a matter of days than that Nina herself was having some kind of breakdown. True, everything she'd experienced lately had *seemed* real . . . but after the past few days Nina didn't trust her eyes, her ears, or even her gut. She didn't know what reality was anymore.

*   *   *

"Oh, this isn't so bad," Nina said aloud in an effort to convince herself.

She looked around her room again. Everything was covered with soot. The walls and floorboards by the door were pretty charred, and there was a puddle on the floor from where the ceiling had dripped water. The floor above Nina had been flooded when an overheated pipe exploded.

It could have been much worse, she reminded herself. The fire had been contained relatively quickly, and the damage to most of the rooms was minimal. Nina and Elizabeth had been able to move back in after just a day; only a few Dickenson residents were still stuck in temporary housing. A flyer taped to Nina's door had informed her that workers would be coming around to take care of any remaining damage over the next couple of weeks.

Nina eyed the brown water stain on her ceiling directly above the puddle. A network of fine lines cracked the plaster where the water had burst through. *It's a good thing I know how much the housing department cares about us,* Nina thought wryly, *or I might suspect that this room is still totally unsafe.*

She reflected that at any other time, she would have been deeply depressed about the state of her room and all her belongings. But right now the possibility that the ceiling might cave in on her head was the least of her problems. *In fact, it might just make all my troubles disappear*, Nina thought glumly as she closed the door behind her and went over to her desk.

The light on the answering machine was blinking. She pushed the button and sat down on her bed, kicking off her shoes. It wasn't even nine o'clock, but since she hadn't gotten much sleep at Steven's, Nina thought she might call it a night soon.

Beep. *"Nina, you're right. We need to talk. Meet me at midnight tonight at Edie's Diner. Please."* Click.

"Was that who I think it was?" Nina bolted up from her bed, hit rewind, and listened to the message again. *Yes, that's definitely Christian's voice*, she realized. *So he does know something!*

A second later the full significance of this revelation dawned on Nina. "I'm not crazy!" she exclaimed giddily. Then she laughed aloud. "Although I am still talking to myself."

She felt elated to learn that she wasn't paranoid. Something was definitely wrong at the experiment, and knowing about it was better than the torture that not knowing had been. Now at least she wouldn't be driven out of her mind by wondering if she was going insane.

But her relief was quickly replaced by apprehension. Now that she was finally going to find out the truth, Nina felt as if she couldn't breathe. *What have I gotten myself into?* she wondered. *Am I really prepared to learn the truth?*

She sat back down on her bed, exhaling deeply. Edie's Diner was a greasy spoon just off campus that was popular with SVU students for no reason other than that it was the only twenty-four-hour diner around. Their coffee was terrible, but Nina had stomached it during finals, and she was prepared to do so again. She just had to kill three hours until midnight.

So much for my early night, Nina thought wearily. *But I can rest* after *I get to the bottom of all this.* There was no way she'd be able to sleep until she talked to Christian anyway.

As he made his way across the moonlit campus Bryan tried to remember if he had always enjoyed the night this much. With the cool breeze on his face, with darkness softening the sharp edges of the buildings and trees, Bryan's senses were heightened. He felt more alive.

And yet if he concentrated hard, Bryan vaguely recalled a time when the sunlight was part of what he liked best about living in southern California. He couldn't remember exactly how long ago that had been. Lately he preferred being in his room or in his cubicle at the psych lab to being out in the sunshine, exposed to its toxic rays. Maybe it was because of watching so much TV, but the harsh light of day hurt his eyes. He didn't like the glare, the bright colors . . . Bryan didn't like what showed up in the light. He felt that he was at his best under cover of night, unseen. There was safety in darkness. Invisibility was invulnerability.

Especially tonight, it was important that he be invisible. Bryan didn't war.t to think about what would happen if he were seen. He shoved his hands into the pockets of his long black leather coat, wincing slightly at the throb of pain in his cut palm.

Why did I even come here? Bryan wondered as Dickenson Hall loomed in his view. But deep down he knew why. All night long his sleep had been troubled by dreams of Nina calling out to him from a sea of flames. Her imploring look had continued to haunt him all day.

The way she looked last night . . . Bryan closed his eyes and pictured Nina's beautiful face against the mesmerizing backdrop of the fire.

He knew in his heart that she was evil. But something about her expression, about the way she'd called his name . . . it kept replaying in his mind, although he couldn't articulate why. It was as if Nina's look, her actions, hadn't fit with the cold, manipulative witch he knew she was. He'd almost convinced himself that the tears in her eyes hadn't been crocodile tears.

151

Bryan leaned against one of the trees that bordered the lawn of Dickenson Hall. He needed to steel himself. He had to make sure once and for all that Nina was actually out to get him, that her tearful pleas to him hadn't been the least bit sincere. Then he wouldn't be tormented by any more dreams of her demonically angelic face.

But I have to be strong. I can't let her manipulate me. I can't fall under her spell. Bryan slumped against the tree, his head pounding. How was he going to judge whether Nina was telling the truth? He used to think he could look into her eyes and know beyond the shadow of a doubt that she was being honest with him. But he didn't dare trust her anymore.

Suddenly the front door of Dickenson Hall opened, and a familiar figure emerged.

Nina! Again it was as if his thoughts had summoned her. *She* must *be an evil presence.*

This is perfect, Bryan thought, following Nina with his eyes as she turned and began walking away from him. *Invisibility—that's the key.*

When Nina had advanced several yards, Bryan began following at a discreet distance, hidden by the line of trees that shadowed the campus walk. He couldn't believe what a perfect opportunity this was to observe Nina unseen. Bryan had a hunch that wherever she was headed this late at night would tip him off as to her true intentions.

Nina, this is my final test of your loyalty, Bryan vowed silently, watching Nina's back as she turned onto a path that led off campus. *If you fail, you no longer exist to me.*

Christian slid breathlessly into the seat across from Nina, a baseball cap pulled low over his face. "Did anyone see you?" he whispered hoarsely. "Did anyone see you come in?" His eyes darted back and forth.

Nina glanced around the room as well. The diner was almost empty except for an elderly couple three booths down, a guy reading the paper in the booth behind her, and a far corner booth full of Sigma brothers loudly discussing the band they'd just seen.

Nina lowered her shoulders so that her face was level with Christian's. "Who would have seen me?" she demanded, trying to keep her voice quiet in spite of her agitation. She'd been anxious half an hour ago when she arrived, and two cups of coffee had done nothing to mellow her out. "Christian, please, just tell me what's going on."

"OK, OK." Christian hung his head and exhaled deeply. Then he looked up at Nina. "Listen, what I tell you can't leave this room. You're in over your head here. I'm sorry I was so harsh today, but I panicked. There are cameras in those cubicles. If Dr. Akre found out I knew anything . . ." He trailed off, swallowing hard, and ran a hand tensely through his long bangs.

"Go on," Nina urged. "I won't say anything to anyone." She stirred her coffee to have something to do with her hands. The suspense was putting her on edge.

Christian took another deep breath. "I didn't know any of this was going on until a couple of days ago." His anguished eyes bored into Nina's. "Dr. Akre never really filled me in on the exact procedure of the experiment—what kind of information we were receiving from the brain, what patterns we were looking for in the brain wave scan, that kind of thing. I didn't think it was my place to ask a lot of questions—some of these genius scientist types can be touchy, you know?"

"Tell me about it," Nina agreed, shuddering at the memory of Dr. Akre's bristly manner.

"But then I noticed what you noticed—that the subjects seemed to be acting different. Dramatically different. So I started thinking about the experiment and wondering whether it was possible that the procedure was somehow designed not just to *monitor* people's brain waves but to *alter* them."

"Brainwashing?" Nina breathed.

Christian nodded grimly. "So I did a little snooping in the lab, and I came across some notes confirming what I suspected. This experiment doesn't just record people's neurological and physiological responses to stimuli. It actually stimulates and *intensifies* those responses. Based on what I read, it appears that the ad agencies that fund EFC are experimenting in stimulating product cravings in viewers."

"So all this is about advertisers trying to make money?" Nina thought back to Kerri gorging herself at the cafeteria and the girl at the library with her grotesque mask of makeup. *They certainly had intense cravings, I guess,* she thought. "But it's gotten so out of control. People are getting hurt. Why would ad agencies want to cause violence?"

"I don't think that was intentional," Christian speculated. "If my theory is correct and Dr. Akre is really stimulating brain activity through televised signals, it's entirely possible that the hostility and violent activity are side effects of overstimulating the adrenal gland. I don't know for sure yet, though, because I haven't been able to figure out exactly how the subjects' brain waves are being manipulated. And I have no idea why you seem to be the only one unaffected, Nina."

"Are you sure I'm *not* affected?" Nina asked anxiously. "With everything that's been going on, I've been worried that *I'm* the one who's paranoid and delusional."

Christian gave her an apologetic smile. "Don't worry, Nina. I've been observing the subjects, and you're not exhibiting any of their behavior patterns. You don't tremble, or rant, or engage in obsessive-compulsive behavior. Physically you don't seem to have lost an abnormal amount of weight or sleep due to the experiment. I apologize again for what I said earlier—believe me, whatever fears you've had lately are completely grounded in reality."

"But how is it that I could be unaffected?" Nina pressed. "Is it possible Dr. Akre is showing me different commercials or something?"

Christian shook his head. "All the TVs in the cubicles are hooked up to the same tape player. You're seeing the exact same ads everyone else is seeing at the exact same moment. In all honesty, I have no idea why you're immune. But I do know one thing—you're a very brave woman, Nina Harper."

Bryan couldn't believe his ears. The pressure in his chest was so strong, he felt as if he were going to explode. It was all he could do not to leap over the booth and strangle that rat Christian with his bare hands. *But invisibility is too important,* Bryan reminded himself. He was more powerful when he remained unseen.

He congratulated himself mentally on his exceptional powers of invisibility while following Nina into the diner. When the door closed behind her, he'd bought a newspaper from the machine outside the diner. Peering through the glass front of the diner, it was easy to see when Nina's attention was occupied by the waitress. Then on his way in Bryan had smoothly swiped a hat from the coatrack by the door, hiding his face and hair. He had to walk the long way around the diner to avoid Nina, but she seemed too preoccupied to notice him slide into the booth behind her. Slouched behind his newspaper, with the hat on, he was the very picture of invisibility . . . contradictory as that was.

Still, if Nina really cared about me, she would have known it was me the moment I walked in. She would have sensed it, Bryan thought angrily.

He sank further into his seat, gripping the newspaper tightly. He could hear the blood pounding in his temples. *Nina makes me so* angry—*I should have known she was up to no good.* Bryan could have kicked himself for considering, even for a second, the possibility that Nina might not be pure evil. He'd come to her dorm hoping to give her a second chance, and what did he find but Nina heading off to spread more lies about Dr. Akre and the experiment.

Not to mention that she happens to be meeting with her special *friend, Christian,* Bryan thought with revulsion. *Who knows how long the two of them have been getting together behind my back,*

157

plotting against me. Well, they deserve each other!

He could feel perspiration beading on his forehead as his blood began to boil. *And to think all this time I believed they were just carrying on a sleazy little affair. If I'd only known it was something much more sickening—something criminal— I'd have blown the whistle on them a long time ago.*

Bryan fought down his anger. It was important that he stay focused, in control. Getting angry at her meant he was letting her have too much power over him. It was for the best that he finally knew the truth about Nina once and for all. Now he could do something about it—now he could get his revenge.

Not revenge, Bryan corrected himself. *Justice. What they're plotting is horribly wrong. It's my duty to stop them.*

And the sweetest part was that being invisible allowed him to listen to Nina and Christian spout their twisted lies freely. Nothing would make him happier than being armed with all the information he needed to expose their wicked plans.

Just sit tight, Bryan told himself. *Soon the right path will be clear.*

"This is insane. I can't believe what I'm hearing," Nina said, holding up her hands. "Does Dr. Akre know about these violent side effects? Does he even care?"

"I don't know," Christian said in a small voice. He was staring down at the Formica tabletop.

"How did *you* get involved in all this anyway?" Nina demanded. "Couldn't you tell there was something fishy going on from the beginning? That Dr. Akre is a real jerk, if you ask me."

For a moment Christian looked as if he were about to cry. "It seemed like such a great opportunity," he said in a choked whisper. "I kept telling myself it was my imagination."

That's exactly what I went through, Nina realized, instantly feeling guilty for berating Christian. "Hey, I'm sorry," she said in a softer tone. "I'm just taking my frustration out on you. I know it's not your fault."

"Thanks, Nina." Christian met her gaze and managed a feeble smile. "You're sweet for saying that. But I know I have to take responsibility for my actions. I *did* notice that Dr. Akre was acting a little shifty, but I ignored it because I was so awestruck by him. I guess I felt like a big man, working with the famous Dr. Charles Akre."

Seemingly regaining his composure, Christian gave a little chuckle. "See, it sounds silly, but I always wanted to be a scientist," he explained. "Other kids worshiped athletes, but I always had posters of Einstein on my wall. I know, I'm the biggest dweeb you've ever met, right?"

"Well, to coin a phrase," Nina began, "people in

159

dweeby houses shouldn't throw stones. I'm a physics major, so I've learned to embrace the geek within."

Christian laughed. "Like I said, Nina, you're a very courageous woman. I admire that in you. Sometime you'll have to give me some lessons in embracing *my* inner geek—I only wish you'd been around in junior high."

"No problem," Nina returned, grinning. "We'll start a support group." For a second she forgot all about the horrifying circumstances that had brought her and Christian to the diner and took in his handsome, chiseled face. She looked deep into his clear green eyes, as thrown by his good looks as she had been the first time she had seen him.

Now is not *the time for flirting,* she told herself, blinking and shaking herself back to the matter at hand. "So tell me, Christian," she began in a brisk, businesslike voice, "how *did* you get involved with Dr. Akre anyway?"

Christian exhaled heavily. "Well, my undergraduate thesis at SVU was about the psychological effects of the media on the individual and on mass consciousness. I analyzed several well-known cases of mass paranoia that were at least partially caused by the media and argued that psychologists need to pay more attention to the media's influence on the average individual's mental health and well-being."

"That sounds like a really interesting topic," Nina

remarked. "So Dr. Akre heard about your paper?"

Christian shook his head. "No. I heard through the psychology department that he was looking for a research assistant for this experiment, so I sent him a copy of my paper. I figured it was a long shot; every grad student in the department had probably applied. But then he called me back. I had to pinch myself to make sure I wasn't dreaming." Christian sighed. "If only I'd known what I was getting into. Nina, I honestly think Dr. Akre is insane. Some of the things he says . . . the way he looks at me sometimes . . ." Christian trailed off, shuddering. "I have no idea what he's capable of. I can't believe I jumped at the chance to work with him."

"You couldn't have known," Nina said reassuringly. She really felt for Christian—he genuinely seemed torn up by the realization that he'd been involved in something so morally wrong. Besides, he reminded Nina of herself in some ways. She'd have been just as thrilled to have her work singled out by a prominent scientist.

"I guess not," Christian conceded. "I just wish I knew what to do now to make everything all right again."

Nina picked up her cup of coffee. "Well, for one thing, we have to get out of the experiment. We both know it's wrong, and I can't stand to be a part of it anymore."

Christian gaped at Nina, his face ashen. "Nina, don't you understand? The only reason I called you and told you all this was to convince you to come *back* and pretend that nothing is wrong." Christian massaged the bridge of his nose with his fingertips. "I wasn't kidding about you being in over your head. These EFC people aren't kidding around. If either one of us, much less both of us, drops out now, they'll know we know something. And then we'll be in danger. Real danger."

Nina opened her mouth, about to protest, but then the full impact of Christian's words hit her. "You mean—"

Christian nodded grimly. "A lot of money has gone into this project from a lot of different special interest groups. There's too much at stake for EFC to let a couple of students get in their way. That's why you *have* to come back to the experiment tomorrow and act like nothing is wrong, Nina. We can't afford to get Dr. Akre's guard up."

Nina shook her head in amazement. "I just can't believe it's as serious as you say it is."

Christian reached across the table and put his hand on hers. "I think it's more serious than either of us realizes," he said gravely. "But I need a little more time to search the lab for concrete evidence. Please, Nina, show up for the experiment tomorrow. You have to help me buy some time. If we work together, this nightmare will be over soon. I promise."

Nina shifted uncomfortably under Christian's intent gaze. She dreaded the thought of going back to the psych lab, of enduring even one more of those sessions strapped into the chair. *And how do I know I won't end up being affected by the brainwashing after all?* she worried. Going along with Christian seemed like too huge a risk.

But if Christian was right, she could be taking a much greater risk by dropping out. At least if she was on the inside, working with Christian, they'd both have a better chance of gathering the information they needed to convict Dr. Akre and whoever else was responsible before anyone realized they were snooping around.

And I'll be able to keep an eye on Bryan, at least from a distance, she mused. Even though Bryan wanted nothing to do with her, she was determined to do everything she could to get through to him. He was brainwashed, and she had to help him. The more she thought about it, the more Nina grudgingly agreed that Christian's plan made sense.

"OK," she said finally. "What do I have to do?"

Bryan waited, hidden behind his newspaper, for a good five minutes after Nina and Christian left the diner. Then he lowered the paper and crumpled it in his hands. Even if he hadn't wanted to keep out of sight, Bryan wasn't sure he could have gotten up and walked out of the diner just then—his ears were ringing so loudly with rage, he didn't think he could walk straight.

Bryan took in several quick gulps of air, trying to calm down. *I knew it all along. Nina doesn't have an honest bone in her body,* he thought with righteous fury. *It's bad enough that she's sneaking around with that scum, telling lies. But now they want to use their lies to destroy Dr. Akre—the only person I know who really cares about me.*

Bryan smiled as he remembered the friendly way Dr. Akre had reached out to him after witnessing his fight with Nina. The professor was a good person—not like Nina and Christian, who were lying about him the way they lied about everything else.

I can't let them smear Dr. Akre with their filthy lies, Bryan thought wildly, his chest constricting. *I have to stop them. I have to stop them before it's too late.*

A sudden burst of adrenaline propelled him up from the booth and toward the door. Bryan tore off the hat and flung it to the floor, then cringed when he realized he'd broken his shield of invisibility. Behind him he could hear people shouting that he had to pay for his coffee. But he had reached the exit—they couldn't touch him now.

"They'll never get me," he muttered. "Never!"

Without looking back Bryan flung open the door of the diner and fled out to the safety of the night.

Chapter
Ten

"Dr. Akre, hi!" Nina called in a bright, sugary voice. She fluttered her fingers in a birdlike little wave, trying to catch the professor's attention as he walked down the crowded hallway of the psych building, separated from Nina by a sea of students emerging from classes.

Nina glanced down at herself one last time to make sure she looked all right. She'd changed clothes before the session, selecting, after much thought, a white cotton ribbed sweater and knee-length plaid skirt ensemble she thought gave her a kind of innocent schoolgirl air. *"Innocent" is definitely the fashion statement I'm going for right now,* Nina thought with a shudder, remembering Christian's dreadful warnings.

Dr. Akre slowed his pace, narrowing his eyes. He looked Nina up and down, then gave her a stiff nod. Then the professor continued down the corridor toward the control room, looking as if he had no intention of stopping to talk to her.

"Oh—I wanted to ask you something if you have a second." Nina casually stepped sideways, blocking Dr. Akre's path down the corridor.

"Actually I'm on my way to the control room to record some notes on today's session," Dr. Akre said in clipped tones. He fidgeted with the collar of his lab coat. Even if he hadn't been short with her, the tension in his body would have sent Nina the signal that he wanted her to move aside and leave him alone.

"Oh, this'll just take a second," Nina insisted breezily. "See, I'm, uh, writing a paper on the . . . the international scientific community. And I figured as long as I ran into you, maybe I could ask you a couple of questions. It would really help me out." She flashed him her best attempt at an earnest, hopeful smile.

Dr. Akre raised one of his dark, gray-streaked eyebrows. "What, exactly, about the international scientific community is the subject of your paper?"

Nina gulped. "Well, it's kind of a biographical study of a few different scientists that, uh, draws some conclusions, based on their work, about the directions science might be headed in today." *That didn't sound too bad, did it?* she wondered.

"I'm sorry, Ms. Harper, but I really don't

think that my biographical information is relevant to a study of science," Dr. Akre said, bristling with barely veiled annoyance. "If you wish to research my work, I'm afraid you'll have to visit the campus library. Now, if you'll excuse me, I have work to do in the control room."

The professor resumed his brisk stride down the hallway, leaving Nina to let out her breath slowly. There was no point in going after Dr. Akre to try to stall him more—he'd know something was up. At least she'd bought a few minutes. She just hoped that had been enough time for Christian to find the evidence he needed in the control room.

As she started walking toward her cubicle Nina wondered whether her performance had been convincing. She wasn't sure how to interpret Dr. Akre's rude brush-off. *Did those dumb questions make him suspicious, or was he just irritated with me for wasting his time?* she wondered. The professor was so antisocial, it was hard to tell.

But Nina was pretty sure she'd ad-libbed nicely. After all, Dr. Akre had no reason to be suspicious of her. *Now, if I can just keep up my innocent act a little longer, we'll get the proof we need to bust him. All this will be over—and maybe my life will be normal again.*

Maybe.

*   *   *

167

Bryan's eyes followed Nina as she walked briskly down the corridor, swinging her hips like she thought she was all that. A wave of profound disgust washed over him. *I can't believe she thinks no one can see through that innocent act,* he thought contemptuously, his face flaming with hot anger as Nina disappeared into the crowd. *Did she really expect to get away with that when I was right behind her, watching her make a fool out of herself with her sickening lies?* He smirked at the thought of how ridiculously easy it was to spy on her unobserved—Nina was so completely wrapped up in herself, she barely noticed what was going on around her.

"Writing a paper—yeah, *right*," Bryan muttered under his breath. The idea that she'd forced Dr. Akre to listen to her inane, transparent questions added insult to injury.

In spite of the rage that fueled him, Bryan's knees felt momentarily weak as the full weight of Nina's wickedness struck him. He slumped against the wall for support, pressing his fevered cheek against its cool surface.

It was easier when I thought all her deceptions and manipulations were just about me, Bryan reflected sadly. *It was painful to know she threw me over for a revolting little fling, but it's a thousand times worse knowing that her flirting was just a ruse to keep me distracted from what was* really *going on.*

A fresh wave of anger washed over him, giving him strength. *I'm not going to let her get away with it,* he vowed, standing up straight. He knew what he had to do.

He took off at a run down the hall in search of Dr. Akre.

"More coffee, sweetie?"

The waitress, a heavily made-up brunette, tilted the pot questioningly.

"Uh, no, thanks." Nina put her hand protectively over the mouth of her mug and looked up at the waitress with a thin smile. "I do have to get to sleep eventually."

The waitress shrugged the pink pouf shoulders of her Edie's uniform and shuffled in her white orthopedic shoes to the next table.

Actually I'm not sure I ever will *get to sleep,* Nina thought, picking up her coffee mug and draining the last sickly sweet sip, where all the sugar had pooled. *I can't remember the last time I was this wired.*

She'd been sound asleep two hours ago, at 2 A.M., when the phone rang. As soon as she blurrily answered the phone Nina heard a voice hiss, "I've figured it out. It's worse than we thought. Meet me at Edie's right away." Then the line went dead.

Recognizing Christian's voice instantly, Nina had dragged herself out of bed into a pair of

169

sweatpants and over to Edie's before her sleep-muddled brain really had a chance to process what was going on.

But after two hours and three cups of coffee, Nina was wide awake and growing more afraid by the moment. Christian still hadn't shown up. And while Nina had racked her brain for every conceivable reason he might have been held up on his way to the diner, she was having trouble coming up with anything convincing. *There's just not that much traffic at four A.M. And I doubt very much that he's having a hard time deciding what to wear,* she thought wryly.

Nina's stomach was in knots, from worry as much as from drinking three cups of stale, bitter coffee in the middle of the night. *Christian sounded so urgent on the phone,* she recalled. *He was about to tell me something crucial . . . something really horrifying. I don't see what could have made him change his mind.*

Unless someone changed his mind for him.

Nina shuddered. As terrifying as the idea was, it was inescapable. Christian had obviously been on his way to meet her when he called. What could have detained him for two hours?

When we met the other night at the diner, he was so afraid that someone would find out what we knew, Nina recalled. At the time it hadn't seemed real to her. Now she was alarmed—for Christian and for herself.

Who could have found out? Nina wondered. *Nobody saw us together.* Maybe Dr. Akre had stumbled on Christian going through his things in the lab.

Or what if he realized that I was trying to stall him yesterday? Nina thought, cold dread creeping down her spine. If her lame questions had aroused Dr. Akre's suspicions, she and Christian could *both* be in danger.

Nina grabbed her gray hooded SVU sweatshirt from the seat beside her and slid out of the booth. She got her wallet from the front pocket of the sweatshirt and left some crumpled bills on the table. Suddenly she couldn't stand another second of waiting in the diner, obsessing about all the possible harm that might have come to Christian . . . and might be in store for her. She wanted to be home in her own bed, even if there was no way she could get back to sleep.

I'll go home and try to relax, Nina decided. *Then I'll talk to Christian tomorrow at the experiment and find out what happened.*

She ignored the voice in her head that asked if Christian would even be there.

Nina leaned against the wall of her cubicle and closed her eyes, feeling a strange mixture of exhaustion and nervous energy. After getting less than four hours of sleep, she didn't have the energy to pace, even though she was feeling even more claustrophobic than usual.

Christian should have been here by now, Nina realized, her eyes flying open. She hadn't seen him in the hall before the session, so she'd decided to wait in her cubicle. But it had been over fifteen minutes. Christian never took more than ten to make his rounds. With every moment she waited, Nina felt the dread she'd experienced early that morning at the diner prickling over her like a cold rain.

Finally the door opened, and a relieved grin stole over her face. "Thank heaven you're—"

She stopped herself; her smile vanished. "What are *you* doing here?" she demanded in a panicked tone. Then, recovering from her surprise, she added more politely, "I mean, where's Christian?"

Dr. Akre stopped where he was hovering in the doorway. His thin lips pressed together momentarily before curling into a self-satisfied smirk. "What kind of a greeting is that, Ms. Harper? You seem to have a lot of bottled-up hostility, if you don't mind my saying so."

Nina flushed with indignation. *I'm not going to let him bully me,* she thought, taking a step forward and folding her arms across her chest.

"Where's Christian?" she repeated, trying to maintain a reasonable air of civility despite the pounding of her heart. "He usually comes around to attach the electrodes."

"Christian?" Dr. Akre uttered the name as if it were a curse in his native language. "I'm afraid I don't know what you're talking about. I've always hooked the subjects up to the equipment myself."

"Christian," Nina repeated again, unable to stop the trembling in her voice. "Your research assistant. Christian Jimenez."

"My . . . research assistant?" Dr. Akre tilted his head back a fraction of an inch and let out a dry wheezing sound that might have been a laugh. "Surely you're joking, Ms. Harper. As I'm sure anyone of sound mind is aware, I am well known for conducting my research in complete independence."

Nina had a strange sense of vertigo, as if the small cubicle were whirling around her. She pressed her back against the wall, unsure if the room suddenly felt very hot or very cold. "But Christian was involved in this—"

"You must be mistaken," Dr. Akre interrupted in a voice that was like ice. His narrowed eyes bored into Nina's; she stared into them as the room spun behind him. "Maybe I didn't make myself clear. The findings of this project are the property of SVU and EFC. I would never compromise their confidentiality with the presence of untrained, unauthorized personnel. I don't know what you imagined, but there is not, and has never been, an assistant involved in this project."

With that, the professor cleared his throat and extended his arm toward the chair in the center of the room. "Now, if you wouldn't mind taking a seat, the other students are waiting to get started."

Nina's first impulse was to bolt from the room. Her whole body was trembling with terror. *But if I run . . . it would be like openly accusing Dr. Akre of doing something awful to Christian and covering it up.* She gulped. *If I run, I could end up like Christian.* Not that Nina had any idea what had happened to him—but she sure didn't want to find out firsthand. *Maybe the best thing for me to do is just play along,* she reasoned.

Slowly she made her way to the chair and sat down. As the glowing blue TV screen filled her vision she did her best to make her face go blank. Recalling the expressions of the brainwashed students, Nina stared straight ahead, focusing on an imaginary point in the distance.

"I remember now," Nina said, trying to keep her voice completely flat and deadpan. "It *was* always you who hooked us up. I must have been imagining things. I think I was thinking of . . . of something I saw in one of the commercials."

"Good, Ms. Harper," Dr. Akre replied with a slight incline of his head. "I'm glad we were able to clear up this little matter."

As Dr. Akre began strapping on the electrodes

174

Nina thought she saw the corner of his mouth twitch with satisfaction. But Nina had no idea what was going through the professor's head at that moment. *Did my questions about Christian make him suspicious that I'm on to him? Or does he just assume I'm brainwashed like the others?*

"Excuse me . . . could I talk to you for a second?"

The young woman whirled around, looking startled by Nina's light tap on her shoulder. Nina herself had to stifle a gasp at the sight of her face. It was the girl Nina had seen making herself up in the mirror of the library bathroom—just days ago, though it seemed like a whole other lifetime.

In the stark light of the psych lab corridor the girl looked like a ghastly shadow of herself. Her dark hair was a tangled mop, and the thick layer of pancake makeup on her face failed to conceal the deep shadows under her eyes. Thick, smudgy circles of black eyeliner, gobs of mascara, and black lipstick accentuated her gaunt, haggard air. She wore a black dress that looked as if it had once fitted her like a glove, but now it hung loosely on her wasted frame.

Nina swallowed hard as the girl turned vacant eyes on her. Hoping that someone else would remember Christian, she had decided to question the other subjects. Maybe someone had seen him since yesterday. If not, then maybe someone would be able to back her up when she reported Christian's disappearance to the authorities.

Now she wasn't so sure this had been a good idea. It seemed like there wasn't a student involved in the experiment, apart from Nina herself, who didn't have the zoned-out, glazed look this girl wore. *Even if the other students remember seeing Christian, would they be reliable witnesses?* Nina wondered.

"I just wanted to ask you a question," Nina said after she overcame her hesitation. "Have you seen Christian around today?"

The girl blinked rapidly. "Is that a trick question?" she asked, a wary edge in her voice.

"No, no, not at all," Nina said hastily. "I just wondered if you had seen Christian; you know, Dr. Akre's assistant. He usually comes around to our cubicles before the session to hook us up, and I didn't see him today."

"What are you talking about? Dr. Akre is the one who comes around to our cubicles." The girl's eyes were blank, uncomprehending. "He runs the experiment by himself. He's a genius. He doesn't need an assistant."

Nina's blood ran cold. "So you're saying you don't remember a graduate student named Christian? Not from the orientation or any of the sessions?"

"No," the girl said hoarsely, her eyes wide

and frightened. Her lower lip trembled as if she were about to cry. "Stop it. Please . . . stop asking me questions."

As she hurried away, Nina spied another student she recognized from the experiment—a short, black-haired guy walking down the hall with his eyes trained on the floor ahead of him.

Swallowing her mounting feeling of hysteria, Nina cut through the crowd of students to reach him. "Excuse me," Nina said breathlessly as she fell into step beside him. He looked up, obviously startled. "I'm sorry to bother you, but I was just wondering if you had seen Christian at all today. I haven't seen him around."

The student's dark eyes were wide and full of fear. "Who?" he asked in a whisper. "Are you messing with my head?"

It's like they've all been programmed, Nina realized with horror. "No, please don't worry—I was just looking for Christian, Dr. Akre's assistant. You haven't seen him, have you?" She wondered if he could detect the note of apprehension she heard in her own voice.

"I don't know," the guy said flatly. "I think you're confused. Dr. Akre doesn't have an assistant." He shook his head at Nina with a look that could have been pity—or disgust. "I have to go now."

As he walked off, Nina's eyes filled with tears.

Am I losing touch with reality, or is it just everyone around me? she wondered. Frantically she scanned the crowd for another student from the experiment. Most of them had probably taken their money and left the building by now.

It seems like there are fewer people involved now anyway, she reflected. The guy with the goatee hadn't been around since the day Elizabeth had been held hostage. And come to think of it, Nina hadn't seen one of the women since that day either. *She probably set the fire in Dickenson,* Nina realized. In which case it made sense that both she and the guy responsible for the attack would be missing.

But are they in jail? Nina wondered. *Or in hospitals? Or did Dr. Akre . . . get them out of the way?* She had no idea. But either way her chances of finding any evidence of Christian's whereabouts—or even of his existence—were getting slimmer by the minute.

Nina gazed around the hallway in desperation. Suddenly her eyes lit on an almost eerily familiar figure: Bryan. He was walking stiffly down the hall, moving in her direction yet not seeming to see her.

It's him, yet it's not him, Nina reflected sadly. *He moves differently, and I know for a fact he talks differently.* Involuntarily a tear slid down her face at the sight of the empty shell Bryan had become.

But if any of the students involved in the experiment would have a reason to remember Christian, Bryan would, she told herself, wiping the tear away with her finger.

As Bryan drew closer Nina positioned herself so that she was blocking his path. "Bryan! Bryan, hi. I really need to talk to you. Please, just hear me out."

Bryan narrowed his eyes when he saw Nina. As he stared silently at her she saw his hands curl into fists at his sides.

"Bryan, I have to ask you a qu—" Nina began uncertainly.

"Stay away from me," Bryan hissed through clenched teeth, cutting her off. "Just keep your sick, twisted lies away from me."

Nina let out a strangled little yelp as Bryan forcefully pushed past her and stormed down the hall. Reflexively she turned to stare after him. Then she saw something that made her blood curdle.

Dr. Akre was standing a couple of yards away. As Nina watched, Bryan strode toward him, and the two men bent their heads together as if sharing a confidence. Once Bryan looked up and glanced over at Nina, then returned his attention to Dr. Akre.

Bryan's conspiring with Dr. Akre now, Nina realized. For a moment she stood frozen where she was. Then she turned and walked slowly down the hallway, willing herself to stay calm and not make any sudden, incriminating movements.

Suddenly she was immensely relieved that she *hadn't* gotten to ask Bryan about Christian—he would definitely have reported it to Dr. Akre, and her cover would have been blown. *As it is, I'm sure he's going to start keeping an eye on me,* she thought, her heart pounding in her throat. *If either of them catches me snooping around, I'm dead!*

As soon as Nina passed through the door to the stairwell she took off running at top speed. Her feet suddenly felt as if they couldn't carry her fast enough. She had to uncover the truth about the experiment as soon as possible—but she had to watch her step in a big way. She couldn't afford to be seen asking any more questions—she'd have to find some other way of getting information without arousing any suspicion.

But Dr. Akre's guard is up now, Nina reminded herself as she raced down the stairs. *And Bryan's too. I'm running out of time.*

Chapter
Eleven

"Nina! What happened to you?" Elizabeth asked with concern, holding open the door to her room. "Come in—can I get you anything?"

Trudging over to Elizabeth's bed, Nina put up her hand weakly. "No, I'm fine, really." She dropped onto the bed with a sigh. "I just haven't gotten much sleep . . . and I'm kind of stressed out."

Elizabeth closed the door behind Nina and sat down on Jessica's bed, facing her friend. *"Kind of stressed out"—that might be an understatement,* Elizabeth thought, surveying Nina's sallow complexion, the dark circles under her eyes, her drawn cheeks. Nina's clothes looked as if she'd slept in them, and her hair was a mess. Her hands twisted anxiously in her lap.

"Liz, I have to tell you something," Nina began hesitantly. "I'm sorry that I haven't confided in you before. And I'm *so* sorry I flipped out on you when you tried to talk to me after the fire. It's just that the whole thing is . . . it just sounds so crazy. I didn't want you to think I was insane."

"Nina, how could I think you were insane?" Elizabeth said soothingly. "I just wish you had come to me sooner instead of keeping it bottled up like that. You know you can talk to me about anything. That's what I'm here for."

Nina shook her head. "This isn't just anything, Liz. It's . . . it's not just about me. It's bigger than that. And I wouldn't even want to get you involved, except I"—she sniffled and wiped away a tear that was sliding down the side of her cheek—"I don't have anyone else to turn to. And I'm so scared, Liz . . . so scared."

I've never seen her sob like that, Elizabeth thought with alarm. Sitting forlornly on the bed with her head bowed and her shoulders slumped, Nina actually looked smaller than usual. It was as if all her natural confidence had been shattered. *What could have done that to her?*

Elizabeth got up and went to sit beside Nina. "It's OK, you can tell me," she said soothingly, putting a comforting arm around Nina's shoulders. "I'll do whatever I can to help you out. And I'm not going to think you're crazy. I promise."

Minutes later Elizabeth sat speechless trying to digest the unbelievable story of what Nina had seen in connection with the experiment: Bryan's hostility, the students' attacks, Christian's mysterious disappearance, and Nina's fears that she herself was in jeopardy.

The idea of people being brainwashed by the experiment *was* a bit far-fetched. She could understand why Nina had hesitated to share her theory. But it wasn't as if Elizabeth hadn't seen the craziness with her own eyes.

Still, Elizabeth couldn't understand why, if Nina's story were true, Nina herself wouldn't have been affected. *Nina's one of the most trustworthy people I know,* Elizabeth reminded herself. *And she's one of the most grounded.* Nina wasn't excitable or gullible; she had never gone in for any kind of conspiracy theory before. And she certainly wasn't crazy, no matter how harried she looked right now. *Nina's my best friend—if she was having some kind of breakdown, I would have seen it coming far in advance.*

"It's an amazing story," Elizabeth admitted finally. "The idea of ad agencies trying to control people's minds to sell products and using SVU students as guinea pigs . . ." She shook her head slowly. "You have to admit, it sounds wild. Although it would make a great piece for WSVU."

"Elizabeth, I don't know if that's such a good idea," Nina said quickly, looking alarmed. "We don't know how far-reaching this conspiracy is.

There might be a lot of powerful people who don't want this information made public. You could be in big trouble if you were perceived as a threat. You could end up like . . ." Nina trailed off, looking down at her hands.

Like Christian, Elizabeth mentally supplied. The thought was sobering.

"Well, I didn't mean that I was about to race over to the station and do a live report," Elizabeth amended. "But if I do say so myself, I'm pretty sure my journalist's skills could come in handy here. We just have to approach this mystery the way I would approach a story."

"Which is how?" Nina looked up at Elizabeth, her face almost pleading.

Elizabeth cupped her hand to her mouth and darted her eyes around as if checking to make sure nobody was listening. "We snoop around," she stage-whispered, as if imparting some great wisdom. Then, dropping her hand into her lap, she continued. "Christian is missing, right? So we do a little background check on him and see what turns up. Maybe we'll find out something that gives us a lead or at least get some names of people who might have known him." She flashed Nina the reassuring smile she'd perfected over years of helping her impulsive, emotional twin out of scrapes.

Nina nodded, her face relaxing slightly. "So

now the truth comes out," she said in a considerably more lighthearted voice.

"What do you mean?" Elizabeth asked. She went over to her desk and turned on her computer and modem.

"Well, everybody thinks you're this bionic Superwoman type—you know, straight-A student by day, crack journalist by night." There was laughter in Nina's voice. "But now I see that deep down you're just a nerd like me—you're merely applying your nerd skills a little more broadly."

"You've found me out." Elizabeth laughed as she sat down in her desk chair. "You were a worthy nemesis, Nina Harper. It's a shame I'm going to have to kill you."

"*Not* funny," Nina said sternly, raising her voice over the staticlike sound of the modem connecting. She got up from the bed and went to stand behind Elizabeth at the desk. "You know, that's one joke I never expected would hit too close to home, but it does."

"You're right. I'm sorry," Elizabeth said sincerely, though she tried to keep her voice light.

Elizabeth typed in her student ID number and password. "OK, I'm on SVU's file server. So we should be able to access a fair amount of information about anyone on campus. Of course, it would be better if we knew Christian's social security number, but I doubt that came up in conversation."

"Actually I got him to spill it during a game of Truth or Dare," Nina said dryly. "No, but his last name is Jimenez." She spelled it aloud. "And he's a grad student in psychology. That's really all I know."

Elizabeth's fingers flew over the keyboard. Behind her she was aware of Nina lowering her head to look over Elizabeth's shoulder. "OK, I'm at the student directory. I'll just do a search through the psych department for him."

She typed in Christian's name and hit return. After a moment a dialogue box popped up, informing Elizabeth that the computer was searching for alternatives to the name she'd entered. Then a list of names appeared on the monitor.

Elizabeth frowned as she scrolled down the screen with her mouse. There was a Christine Jimson, a Chris Ramirez, and a few other names that sounded only vaguely like Christian's.

"He's not here," Elizabeth said, trying to sound more casual than she felt. The search protocol was a standard one she'd run a million times, and it had always returned the information she needed. She racked her brain for an explanation that wouldn't alarm Nina. "The search must have been too specific. Maybe I only went through the undergraduate psych department. Here, I'll try searching the entire university directory." She went back several screens to the main university

186

directory, then entered Christian's name again.

This time a longer list of alternatives appeared. But there was no Christian Jimenez among them.

Elizabeth leaned back in her chair. She and Nina studied the screen for a moment without speaking.

"Maybe he goes by his middle name or something," Nina suggested. "Try just entering 'Jimenez' and see what comes up."

Elizabeth shook her head. "The search would have given us every possible alternative even if one whole word didn't match." She pointed at a name on the list. "See, there's even a Professor Jorge Jimenez in the art history department." She licked her lips nervously and turned to face Nina. "Nina, I don't know what to tell you. This is the master SVU directory. If Christian isn't on this list, either that wasn't his real name, or he wasn't really a student here."

"But that's impossible. I just don't believe he was lying. Why wouldn't he have told me when we met at the diner?" Nina slowly backed away from the computer, looking stunned, and half sat, half fell back onto Elizabeth's bed.

Elizabeth turned back to her screen, frowning. "Is there anything else you can think of to search for? Any campus organizations he belonged to? Awards? Publications?"

Nina snapped her fingers. "What about a thesis? Is there any way we could track down one of those?"

"Well, the SVU libraries keep a copy of all student theses on file," Elizabeth said. "They're a great resource when you don't have a lot of time to do research. Why, did he talk to you about his thesis?"

Nina nodded. "It was on psychology and the media. He said he analyzed incidents of mass paranoia."

Elizabeth clicked her mouse to return to the main SVU directory. "OK, let me just get into the main library database and I'll run a keyword search."

For a few minutes Elizabeth was silent as she logged in to the SVU libraries. "Now I'm going to search for *psychology* and *media*," she told Nina over her shoulder, typing in a string of commands.

"Anything?" Nina asked in a high, tight voice.

Elizabeth shook her head again. "I tried searching in the psychology theses for media, paranoia, and Christian's name again. We got a paper on the psychology of the paranormal, but nothing about Christian's thesis." She turned back to Nina. "I know it's hard to believe, but it looks like Christian wasn't telling you the truth. If he wrote that thesis, it would be here—just like he would be in the records if he were a student at SVU."

"But it's not like that!" Nina insisted. "I know it sounds crazy, Liz, but Christian wasn't lying—the records are! This can't be an accident.

Somebody wants to make it seem like he never existed at all. Don't ask me how . . . I don't know. I don't know anything anymore."

She buried her face in her hands, sobbing. "Liz, I feel like I'm losing my mind. It's hopeless—if I can't figure out something soon, they're going to kill me!"

"Nina, don't talk like that! You can't give up now. We still have other leads to go on."

Nina lifted her tear-streaked face from her hands. "Like what?" she asked dubiously.

"Well, we can look up some other names—Dr. Akre's or that corporation you said was funding the experiment," Elizabeth suggested. "The clue we need could be in the SVU computer network or on the Internet—who knows. But I mean, you can't just concede defeat when there's so much more we can do without even leaving this room."

Nina shook her head exhaustedly, wiping away the last of her sudden outburst of tears. Elizabeth Wakefield's boundless confidence in the triumph of right over wrong never ceased to amaze her. *Still, Liz has come through for me more than once when she's in her crusader mode,* Nina admitted to herself. She recalled how, early in the school year, Elizabeth had worked tirelessly to expose the racist perpetrators of an assault on Nina and Bryan. Nina had been ready to give up then—in fact, she'd been so unsettled by the attack that she had planned to leave SVU and move back home. But Elizabeth had helped her see that running away would only give the hate mongers exactly what they wanted—*and* allow them to go on terrorizing minority students.

She was right then, and she's right now, Nina realized suddenly. Even if she ignored her conscience entirely, the facts spoke for themselves. Christian had already disappeared off the face of the earth, and she could very well be next. Not to mention that Bryan might as well have disappeared too, for all there was left of the bright, caring, principled man she'd once known. As long as she was still alive, she had to fight to save Bryan from the brainwashing that had transformed him.

"You have a point, Liz," Nina said finally. She managed a smile, hoping to convince herself as well as Elizabeth that she felt optimistic. "I mean, the combined force of our geek power has to be more or less unstoppable. If research is the answer, two people who have logged as many hours in the library as we have should be able to solve any problem that comes our way."

"Now you're talking." Elizabeth grinned at Nina, then turned back toward the computer. "OK, where do I start? With Dr. Akre or the corporation?"

Nina's brows knit. "I have a feeling Dr. Akre doesn't exactly have a great PR team. He seems to be pretty defensive about personal information. So maybe you should try looking up EFC."

"OK, I'll get onto the Web and search for information," Elizabeth said. She moved the mouse and typed something short. From the bed Nina saw the display on the monitor change. Curious, she got up and stood behind Elizabeth again.

As Nina watched, Elizabeth entered the World Wide Web address of a search engine and typed in *EFC* as the object of the search. When she hit return, a new page covered with text appeared on the screen.

"So these are all the Web pages that mention EFC?" Nina asked, frowning with confusion. "I don't see a site that's maintained by the company itself."

"Me either," Elizabeth said, scrolling down with the mouse. "It's weird that a corporation funded by ad agencies wouldn't promote itself in every possible way. Web sites are such a cheap form of advertising—practically every company has one these days."

"So what are all these sites?" Nina asked. Most of them had long, complicated addresses that didn't include EFC in any way.

"They look like people's home pages," Elizabeth answered, clicking on one name to link to the page. "Let's find out what they have to do with EFC."

As Elizabeth's computer loaded the page, the first thing Nina saw was a huge headline that read Phil Roper's Conspiracy Theory Home Page. Then a picture of a geeky-looking college-age guy appeared.

"That must be Phil," Nina remarked.

Elizabeth scrolled down the page as screen after screen of text loaded. "Listen to this," she said excitedly. "'One of the most persistent conspiracy theories in the past ten years involves a market-research corporation known as EFC, which claims to receive its funding from a variety of advertising agencies. But these "ad agencies" reputedly filter money from'—get this—'the military-industrial complex, through a network of subcorporations, to conduct "research" that actually consists of experiments in mass paranoia.'"

Nina felt as if the temperature in the room had suddenly dropped about thirty degrees. "Mass paranoia," she echoed in a whisper. "Just like Christian's thesis!"

"'EFC's experiments allegedly seek to establish a method through which mass media can accomplish mind control on a large scale,'" Elizabeth continued. "'The exact purpose of EFC's supposed illegal experimentation is hotly debated among conspiracy theorists. . . .' Oh, Nina, this is just some guy's idea of being clever. I mean, could that be any more vague?"

"Try another page," Nina urged. "See if we find anything else like that."

Elizabeth went back to the page of search results and clicked on another address. A page popped up labeled The 100 Greatest Conspiracies of Our Time.

Nina sucked in her breath. "It's another conspiracy page! See if you can find what it says about EFC."

"I'm getting to it," Elizabeth replied, sounding a little tense. "Huh! It's number twenty-seven. Not a bad showing. Check this out." She pointed to a line of text on the monitor. "Start here."

Nina leaned in to read the words on the screen. She quickly scanned a paragraph stating information similar to what they'd read on the first Web page. Then her eyes traveled farther down the page.

EFC also has a reputation for "disappearing" individuals who attempt to expose its corruption. If the rumors are true, EFC's connections are far-reaching enough that the corporation can effectively wipe out every physical and bureaucratic trace of a person's existence if they fear that person poses a threat to their "research." Of course, this insistence on EFC's ability to wipe out all records of their own activity may just be an excuse on the part of conspiracy theorists to explain their own lack of evidence.

"'Disappeared'—that must be what happened to Christian!" Nina exclaimed aloud, her eyes filling with hot tears. "They killed him . . . and then they hacked into the school's computers and wiped out every trace of his existence."

"Nina, you can't be serious." Elizabeth turned to face her friend in disbelief. "This isn't evidence—we're just looking for leads. A million different crackpots have home pages on the Internet so they can spout their outrageous theories to get attention. The Web's not regulated at all, and nobody ever credits their sources, so it's not a reliable source of information. I mean, do you really think it's plausible that such a massive, far-reaching conspiracy could exist?"

"But Liz, it fits too perfectly with everything that's happened," Nina argued, rubbing her eyes. "It always seemed odd that this whole thing was about ad agencies—that they would be giving funding to a university in the first place, and then that they would actually put lives at risk to sell products. It makes sense that something much more sinister is going on. That the students becoming paranoid wasn't just a side effect but the actual *point* of the experiment. Maybe that's what Christian was trying to tell me before he . . ."

"Disappeared?" Elizabeth furnished. A chill crept up her spine.

Her rational mind told her that Nina was definitely jumping to conclusions. *But my gut says Nina has a point,* she thought, shivering with fear. *The theory* does *fit with everything we've seen.* Whatever had happened to Bryan and to that guy at the snack bar . . . it was obviously about more than just subliminal advertising.

Nina nodded gravely. "It sounds crazy to me too, Liz. But you have to admit, it's all consistent."

Elizabeth gave her a crooked smile. "It's not like crazy things haven't been happening lately. I'll take a look at a couple more of these pages." She turned back to the monitor.

As Elizabeth clicked on the names of several different Web sites the same information about EFC kept appearing. Not one of the sites that had come up in her search mentioned EFC in its capacity as a research firm for ad agencies. All of them appeared to be devoted to conspiracy theories.

"Nina, I just want you to understand that this still doesn't prove anything," Elizabeth said after they had examined over a dozen Web pages. "One of the most annoying things about the global village is that rumors spread like wildfire. I believe you when you say something strange is going on, but it just doesn't seem possible that all these accusations are true. The fact that you're unaffected . . . it just doesn't add up."

"I know it doesn't make sense," Nina conceded. "But I know what I've seen—and what you've seen too." She met Elizabeth's eyes. "I wouldn't believe it if I hadn't experienced it firsthand. But I honestly think SVU students are being used as guinea pigs for this horrible mind-control plan. Maybe if we find out how Dr. Akre is controlling the students, we'll understand why it's happening to everyone but me. Please, Liz, even if you're not totally convinced . . . I really need your support on this. I can't do it alone."

"Of course I'll help you, Nina," Elizabeth promised. "I want to get to the bottom of this almost as much as you do. I'm just saying that the simplest explanation is usually the correct one. Maybe EFC isn't what it appears to be, but lots of corporations keep quiet about where they get their funding. It doesn't mean they're experimenting with mind control."

"I know," Nina said, sighing. "I think the theory is pretty out there too. But it's the only way I can make sense of everything that's happened, especially Christian's disappearance." She twirled one lock of her unruly dark hair around her finger. "If only we could find out what exactly is going on in that lab, we'd know what Christian was trying to tell us. We'd know how the students are being brainwashed. . . ."

"And why you're unaffected." Elizabeth nodded sharply, still unsure of what, exactly, Nina's being "unaffected" entailed. "OK. Count me in."

Chapter Twelve

"Smoke. Burn, smoke, burn. Fire. Burn. *Get them off me!*"

Nina stared at the floor as she made her way down the hall, concentrating on keeping her face blank and shuffling down the corridor as slowly as the other students. She tried hard not to pay attention to the steady mutterings of the young man walking ahead of her—she didn't need the distraction or the strain on her jangled nerves right now.

Dr. Akre led the motley band of students to their cubicles for the day's session, his arms laden with videotapes. Nina was hanging back at the end of the line, trying to look inconspicuous. Even though the professor had his back to her, she figured it couldn't hurt to practice blending in with the brainwashed subjects. Her safest bet was for the other students, as well as Dr. Akre, to get the impression Nina was one of them; for all she knew, Bryan might not be the only one in the professor's confidence.

She stole a glance toward Bryan, who was walking side by side with Dr. Akre. Their heads were together, and they were talking softly. The sight made Nina nervous; then again, just being in the creepy psych lab surrounded by this volatile group of students put her on edge.

"Burn, smoke them out," mumbled the guy in front of Nina, lifting an arm to wave desultorily at the air around his head. Nina saw long raised scabs on his forearm and realized he was the guy who had scratched himself up so badly before. It was getting harder to tell the zombielike subjects of the experiment apart.

Maybe it was a mistake to come back here, Nina mused. After she had confronted Dr. Akre the other day, Nina wasn't sure it was safe. Yet when she showed up staring into space and shuffling her feet like the other students, Dr. Akre hadn't batted an eye.

As long as he seems convinced that I'm under his spell like the others, I'm better off staying, Nina reminded herself. *If I drop out now, I'll blow my chance to pick up any evidence—not to mention mark myself for death.*

Still, the atmosphere at the lab had become even more strained since Christian had disappeared. The students flocked behind the professor like sheep, but at the slightest provocation—a loud noise, a sudden movement—they were capable of rearing like frightened horses. By himself Dr. Akre had a hard time keeping them under control. He'd had to restrain hysterical students twice already.

I've got to find a way to use the chaos to my advantage, Nina resolved.

Several feet ahead of her the guy ran his fingers frantically through his short brown hair, continuing to mutter and occasionally give a little yelp.

The group had almost reached the cubicles when the guy in front of Nina let out a piercing scream. The students turned around to see the young man drop to the floor and start rolling around, kicking with his feet. His arms tore at his shirt. "Get them off me!" he howled. "Burn them off!"

A murmur ran through the little throng of students. Someone let out a shriek of fear. Nina glanced over and saw Dr. Akre making his way through the crowd, hurrying toward the student who lay thrashing on the floor. "Calm down, please!" he begged. "Everybody, please remain calm!"

In his haste the professor jostled a student in the crowd, and Nina saw one of his videotapes fall to the floor.

As Dr. Akre reached down, struggling to grab

hold of the student's wrists, his back was turned. Instantly Nina saw her chance. Quickly stepping behind Dr. Akre, she knelt and slipped her backpack off her shoulder. After glancing up to make sure she was unnoticed, she unzipped her backpack and stuffed in the tape. As she zipped the pocket back up and got to her feet, Nina put on the spaced-out poker face she'd copied from the brainwashed students.

Around her students were whimpering and beginning to drift around in the hallway. The guy on the floor was still screaming. Dr. Akre wrestled to pull him to his feet, calling out to the other students to stay calm and remain where they were.

No one saw me, Nina realized, although her heart was pounding so loudly, she was surprised Dr. Akre didn't hear it. *I can't believe I got away with it!* She exhaled deeply, trying to expel the adrenaline rush of fear and exhilaration that flooded her, and fought to flatten out the tiny smile of triumph that twitched at the corners of her lips.

But she felt like laughing out loud. This was the break she'd been waiting for. Finally she had some evidence.

Elizabeth hit pause and looked closely at the screen to make sure she had the shot she wanted.

A middle-aged man in a suit was frozen with his lips flared into an unnatural midspeech grimace. Elizabeth advanced the picture a few frames until his mouth closed, then made a note of the time code on her legal pad. She shifted in her black vinyl chair and checked her watch. Almost five. She'd been sitting in WSVU's editing room for nearly two hours, screening interviews with members of the SVU administration, and she still hadn't found any really great footage. Impatiently Elizabeth held down the fast-forward button, hoping to see some facial expression or arm gesture that would signal an interesting sound bite. But this guy was as dry as toast. He sat with his hands folded in his lap and occasionally pressed his thumbs together. Not exactly the media event of the century.

As she fast-forwarded through the next few minutes of the tape Elizabeth felt a twinge of guilt that she wasn't being as much of a perfectionist as usual. Normally she would have spent days, not hours, editing this story—it was scheduled to run as a special feature on the next night's WSVU news broadcast. But tonight Elizabeth couldn't focus her mind on the administration's changes in student financial aid policy. She hadn't been able to stop thinking about the crazy theory she and Nina had unearthed yesterday. All Elizabeth's instincts told her there was a major story there, even if the far-fetched rumors they'd read on the Web weren't true.

The sooner I concentrate on finishing this edit, the sooner I can get home and start looking for more information, Elizabeth reminded herself. Not only was she holding out hope that she'd eventually be able to break the EFC story on WSVU without endangering herself and Nina, she was afraid of what might happen if the terror was allowed to continue on campus. Her life had already been jeopardized more than once.

Elizabeth let go of the fast-forward button, and the tape slowed to normal speed. She leaned back in her chair, focusing on the man in the suit and the standards by which he judged SVU applicants for financial aid. Summoning her powers of concentration, Elizabeth watched intently, occasionally scribbling notes on her pad. After several minutes had gone by, a knock at the door interrupted her. Elizabeth pressed stop and called out, "It's open!"

The door opened and Nina appeared, flushed and breathless, a wide grin lighting her face. She looked a lot more pulled together than when Elizabeth had last seen her. Her hair was clipped neatly back in silver barrettes, and she was wearing a short charcoal blazer and black jeans that gave her a confident, take-charge air.

"Liz, I'm so happy I caught you here. I just came

from the experiment, and I really need your help."

"Whatever you look so psyched about, I'll make time for," Elizabeth said eagerly, glad for the distraction. "What's up? Any news?"

"Check this out." Nina took off her backpack, unzipped it, and triumphantly produced an unmarked videotape. "One of the subjects freaked out today at the session, and Dr. Akre dropped this in the commotion. I bet it's one of the tapes of commercials they show us. That's why I wanted to find you here—to see if we could examine it for any kind of subliminal signals."

"Quick thinking, Nina!" Elizabeth exclaimed when Nina came over and handed her the tape of commercials. "You came to the right place— WSVU's editing equipment is totally cutting edge. If there are any hidden messages in this tape, we'll find them." She examined the tape. "Half inch. Regular old VHS. We'll need this machine over . . . here." She pushed the tape in the VCR and flipped the input switch attached to monitor A. "Now we're cooking. Grab a chair."

"Thanks, Liz," Nina said, dragging a chair over from a nearby desk. "But listen, I'm not sure it's such a good idea for you to watch the tape with me. What if you're affected by it? We still don't know why I'm immune."

Elizabeth hesitated with her finger poised on the play button. "I hadn't thought about that."

She turned to Nina. "But one tape isn't going to drive me totally out of my mind, right? If I start to feel weird, I just won't watch anymore."

"OK, but be careful," Nina said, sounding worried. "I already feel guilty about dragging you into this. I'd never forgive myself if anything . . . happened to you."

"Let's try not to think about it." Elizabeth shuddered, recalling the glazed, soulless looks of the guy she'd thought was a druggie, the man in the snack bar, and Bryan. Before she could change her mind, she hit play and leaned back in her chair.

A box of doughnuts appeared on the screen; as Elizabeth and Nina watched, the girl holding the box picked out a doughnut and bit into it.

"Not exactly inflammatory stuff," Elizabeth commented, aiming her remote control.

"Wait until you've watched two hours of it," Nina cautioned as Elizabeth rewound the scene and then replayed it frame by frame. "You might feel like attacking somebody too."

Three and a half hours later Elizabeth was ready to concede Nina's point. Her eyes ached, her neck was stiff, and her left leg was asleep. Not to mention that she was starving, since she hadn't eaten since lunch. She and Nina had played the tape forward and backward, frame by frame, at double speed, at half speed, and with every other manipulation Elizabeth could think of. And they'd found nothing.

"Well, I'm stumped," Elizabeth admitted finally. "If there's anything out of the ordinary encoded into these ads, it's not something our equipment can pick up."

"Maybe the signals aren't actually recorded on the tape," Nina suggested. "Maybe they're transmitted some other way. Is there anything else we can check for?"

Elizabeth shook her head wearily. "Not that I can think of. But I'll make a dupe of the tape just in case. I assume you want to return the original as soon as possible, before Dr. Akre notices it's missing."

"Definitely," Nina agreed. "Thanks, Liz, I really appreciate it. Sorry this was so frustrating."

"Don't worry about it. Even finding nothing on the tape helps us rule out some possibilities. Like you said, maybe the messages are being sent some other way."

Elizabeth stood up, shifting her weight from one side to the other to get the blood flowing back through her legs. "I'll take another look at the tape tomorrow in case there's anything I'm not thinking of. But right now I think we both need to get out of this room, get some fresh air, and grab something to eat before we pass out."

* * *

"I don't think pasta ever tasted so good to me before," Nina said contentedly, resting her hand on her full stomach. "I'm kind of glad the cafeteria was closed—it was much nicer to go to La Dolce Vita. I didn't even realize until we got there that I haven't really eaten much in the past few days. For once stress has made me *lose* my appetite."

"I wish I had that problem." Elizabeth groaned. "When I'm stressed out, my first impulse is to reach for a cookie."

"Well, maybe that's not always a bad thing," Nina mused, exhaling contentedly. "I know I feel a lot more relaxed right now, after a good meal. Although I don't know if I really expect to get much studying done later—I have a feeling I'm just going to collapse when I get back to my room."

"That sounds tempting." Elizabeth sighed. "I have *so* much work, though."

Nina nodded absently, savoring the first feeling of peace she'd experienced in days. The night was warm, and the quad was filled with students strolling in couples or groups. Many were dressed up, like they were headed out on dates or to parties.

It's Friday night, Nina realized with a start. *The weekend.* She felt a twinge of sadness at the thought that ordinarily she'd have had a date—at the very least a study date—with Bryan. It was depressing to see so many people out having fun when her life had fallen apart. But at least she felt safer being out at night with the campus so busy and alive.

"Are you OK, Nina?" Elizabeth asked, turning to face her. "You looked kind of preoccupied for a minute there."

"I'm fine," Nina answered, smiling thinly. "I was just thinking about . . ."

Suddenly she trailed off. Her face fell. A few feet ahead of them was Kerri, looking disheveled in a torn long-sleeved shirt, a long coat, and rumpled pajama bottoms. She was walking across the quad in unsteady half circles and mumbling to herself.

She's headed our way, Nina realized uneasily. *That's not a good sign.* Ever since the day Kerri attacked the football player and accused Nina of plotting against her, Nina had steered clear of her. There was no telling what Kerri would do if Nina crossed her path.

Nina took hold of Elizabeth's arm, intending to steer her out of Kerri's way. But as she leaned in to guide Elizabeth off to the side she accidentally stepped on Elizabeth's foot.

"Ow!" Elizabeth exclaimed. "What are you trying to do, run me over?"

At the sound of her voice Kerri whirled around. Her eyes blinked uncomprehendingly for a moment. Then they locked in on Nina's face and narrowed into slits.

208

Nina cringed. "Um, Kerri—hi! Sorry if we startled—"

"*You!*" Kerri hissed. She had stopped dead in her tracks, her feet planted firmly in Nina and Elizabeth's path. "I knew you were after me! How long have you been following me?"

Nina put her hands up, palms out, as if to deflect Kerri's fury. "Nobody's following you, Kerri. We were just on our way back from—"

"Shut up!" Kerri screeched. Her shrill voice echoed across the campus. In the distance Nina saw a few heads turn with surprise in their direction. "I know you're lying! You want to kill me *dead*. . . . Well, it's not going to happen!"

All at once Nina felt as if she were standing outside herself, watching the scene unfold in slow motion like a movie. Kerri reached inside her coat. Nina's mouth opened and formed a soundless *no*. Beside Nina, Elizabeth's hands flew to her face.

And then, in a split second that seemed to last forever, Kerri pulled out a gun. Gripping it in both her uncontrollably trembling hands, she aimed it straight at Nina.

Chapter Thirteen

This can't be happening, Elizabeth thought, staring hypnotized at the snub-nosed revolver Kerri was aiming unsteadily at Nina. It was like a nightmare she couldn't wake up from. *Are we really going to die like this?* she wondered, a lump welling in her throat. There were so many things she wanted to do and see in her life. Now, if she made one false move, all that could be cut short.

Elizabeth glanced around, desperately searching for an escape route or someone to come to their rescue. The quad, where moments ago students had been strolling peacefully, had suddenly come alive with students screaming and running for cover. Kerri jerked the gun upward and fired a shot into the air. "Don't move!" she shrilled, lowering the gun back down toward Nina. "Everybody be quiet!"

Most of the people on the quad froze where they were. But one young man in a gray dress jacket and tie tried to take off through the crowd. Kerri spotted him and, narrowing her eyes even further, swung the gun around. She fired a shot that caught him in the back of the leg.

Elizabeth gasped as the guy went down, screaming. His date, a curvy blond in a long white dress, knelt by his side, screaming hysterically. As she caught him up in her arms Elizabeth saw blood splatter the woman's dress. As the dark stain on the guy's pant leg spread, Elizabeth involuntarily put her hand to her heart. *Crazy as this girl is, she managed to hit that guy from fifty feet away,* she realized. *If she shoots me or Nina, it won't be in the leg.*

Elizabeth looked back at Kerri, whose eyes widened as she stared at the guy moaning in pain on the ground. The fear those eyes held—as if Kerri thought she were the hunted instead of the hunter—made Elizabeth flash back to the guy at the snack bar. He'd worn the same look of terror and helplessness.

Suddenly that mass paranoia theory doesn't sound so ridiculous, Elizabeth realized, an icy shudder running through her.

"Shut up!" Kerri screamed at the man she had shot before turning the gun back on Nina. "Nobody talk. Nobody move. Nobody breathe!"

As if from very far away, Elizabeth heard the

screams of the wounded man and his girlfriend quiet to frightened whimpers. But her eyes remained fixed on Kerri, whose hands were still shaking violently. *She seems so unstable, so unsure of herself,* Elizabeth thought desperately. *There must be a way to talk her down.*

Slowly Elizabeth took a step back. She saw Kerri's eyes dart toward her. Then, before she knew it, the gun was pointed right at her.

Elizabeth's knees went weak. The barrel of the gun, swaying in uneven circles in Kerri's trembling grip, was all she could see. *She's going to shoot me!* Elizabeth thought desperately, fighting to keep her terror from showing on her face. She forced herself to summon all her wits. *If we can at least stall her, maybe the police will show up,* she thought hopefully.

"Please don't hurt us," Elizabeth whispered in as gentle and soothing a voice as she could muster. She lifted her hands in a gesture of surrender. "We don't want to hurt you. Please don't be afraid."

"Who are you?" Kerri cried in a strangled voice, her bloodshot gaze flitting up and down Elizabeth's body. "You're after me too! What did she tell you?"

"I didn't tell her anything," Nina called out. In a flash Kerri swung the gun back toward Nina.

For a moment, as Kerri turned away from her, Elizabeth felt strangely removed, as if she were watching the scene unfold from a distance. As the gun teetered back and forth it reminded Elizabeth of a pendulum, ticking off a second with each swing. *Is it counting out the last moments of our lives?* Elizabeth found herself wondering. She closed her eyes for a moment, trying to memorize every last sense impression—the scent of the warm California night air, the soft lawn beneath her feet, the thudding of her heart.

I'm not ready to die! Elizabeth's eyes flew open as the realization struck her with sudden force. She glanced over at Nina, who was locked into a staring contest with Kerri. *Be careful, Nina!* she implored her friend silently. *Don't do anything that will get you killed!*

"She's not after you," Nina insisted, lifting her hands in surrender as Elizabeth had. "We both just want to help you. Please calm down, Kerri. You don't have to be afraid."

Elizabeth saw Nina risk a sideways glance over at her. Elizabeth inclined her head slightly to show that she had the same idea. Her heart was pounding wildly, but she struggled to keep calm. *If she senses how scared I am, she'll shoot us for sure,* she thought, mentally willing herself to gather every ounce of concentration she possessed.

"Please put the gun down, Kerri," Elizabeth called, her voice echoing across the eerie, charged silence of the crowded quad. "I know you don't want anybody to get hurt."

As Kerri swung the gun back toward Elizabeth, Nina chimed in, "Put the gun down." Almost reflexively Kerri lurched back around toward Nina. Her eyes darted back and forth uncertainly between Nina and Elizabeth.

It's working—she doesn't know what to do! Elizabeth realized, her heart fluttering. Kerri looked frightened and vulnerable, like a deer caught in headlights. *But how long can we keep stalling?* It was dangerous to keep pushing Kerri's buttons, throwing her off guard. At any moment she might panic and pull the trigger.

Nina, please think of something, Elizabeth silently begged her friend. *We're too young to die!*

Nina licked her lips. Kerri's huge, glazed eyes, full of hatred and incomprehension, bored steadily into her. But the gun still wavered, betraying Kerri's nervousness and confusion. "Kerri, please don't do anything you might regret," Nina begged.

"Shut up," Kerri whispered. "Don't tell me what to do!"

Nina choked back a sob as Kerri cocked the gun. *This is it,* she thought despairingly. *I'm going to die. Without even getting to say good-bye to the people I love.*

Nina risked a glance over toward Elizabeth.

Their eyes met for an instant, and Nina saw her own terror reflected in her best friend's face. They exchanged sad, fleeting smiles of sympathy; then Nina turned her attention back to Kerri.

"Look at me, Nina!" Kerri cried. "I know what you're up to, but it's not going to work, do you hear me? I'll see you dead first!"

Just then Nina saw a blur of movement behind Kerri. She strained to make out what it was without appearing to unfocus her attention from Kerri's face. When she realized what was happening, she wanted to sob with relief. Emerging from behind buildings and bushes were swarms of armed police officers. Nina's heart surged with new hope, and she had to strain to keep her face expressionless.

But it's not over yet, Nina reminded herself. If Kerri panicked at the sight of the cops, Nina and Elizabeth could be dead meat.

"Kerri," Nina heard Elizabeth say. "Please don't do this."

Nina glanced toward the sound of Elizabeth's voice. Elizabeth had taken a few discreet steps back and was holding her hands up in a gesture of surrender.

Kerri turned to point the gun at Elizabeth. Then she shook her head as if doing a double take and turned toward the police officers assembled in the bushes and on the ground. It took a few beats for her face to register recognition. "Oh no!" Kerri screeched in an anguished tone. Her head twisted spastically back and forth, as if she were trying vainly to keep all the police officers in her sights. "You sent them to get me!" She staggered backward, lowering the gun for a second.

Before Nina realized what she was doing, she lunged at Kerri with every last ounce of strength she had. Her hands closed over Kerri's wrists, straining to wrest the gun away. Kerri held on tight.

"No!" Kerri shrieked in a bloodcurdling voice. "I'll get you before you get me!"

The two of them swayed together, Nina grasping Kerri's wrists and Kerri trying to squirm out of Nina's hold. Every fiber of Nina's being was focused on keeping her hands locked on Kerri's.

Just then Nina felt Kerri's foot come down hard on hers. Involuntarily Nina gasped in pain, and her grip on Kerri's wrists loosened slightly. With a cry Kerri strained to wrench her arms away. Nina felt her grasp slipping. In another second Kerri would be free!

Just as her hands slipped, Nina felt herself being pulled from Kerri in a tidal wave of blue-uniformed bodies. She saw Kerri's gray eyes grow enormous as an officer karate-chopped the back of her wrist, causing the gun to fly from her hand. Another officer retrieved the gun as Kerri's hands were cuffed behind her back.

Suddenly the darkened quad was alive with lights and sirens. All Nina could see was a black, white, and blue blur of figures in motion. Beyond the throng of cops people were screaming and crying.

Then, from the haze of shadowed faces, bright lights, and distant cries, a solid and familiar figure emerged. "Nina!" Elizabeth cried, flinging her arms around Nina's neck. Nina hugged her back, tightly. "Thank goodness you're OK! You saved my life."

"You mean I *risked* your life." Nina pulled back from Elizabeth's embrace. The tears that moments ago she had been too petrified to shed now came flooding forth. "You'd never have been involved in this nightmare if it hadn't been for me. I don't know what I was thinking, dragging you into—"

"Nina, stop it." Elizabeth cut her off, squeezing her shoulders. "Stop blaming yourself. You didn't drag me into this—I wanted to help you. I wanted to find out the truth. And you know what else?"

"What?" Nina asked, her lip still quivering with sobs.

Elizabeth looked her right in the eyes. "I believe you, Nina."

"What?" Nina croaked through her tears, wiping her nose on the cuff of her blazer. "You do?"

Elizabeth nodded seriously. "I know I was

217

skeptical at first. . . ." She shook her head. "But this is no conspiracy theory. Somebody wants these people to panic like this. Somebody powerful enough to know the value of panic . . . and influential enough to use chaos to their advantage."

Bryan's footsteps echoed through the silence of the stairwell. Winding his way down the stairs in complete darkness, listening to the sound of his steps go on forever, Bryan felt his head singing with exhilaration, as if he were in a kind of transcendent state. *I can't remember the last time I felt so alive,* he thought almost blissfully.

I've arrived, Bryan thought, pushing open the door to the psych lab basement. *I know what I have to do.* He tried to recall whether, earlier at the session, Dr. Akre had whispered in his ear to come here, or whether he had just *known*. Either way it didn't matter. His destiny was at hand.

The basement was a huge, dark room full of hulking shadows and reeking of mildew. The entire high-ceilinged space glowed a faint green from the far corner, where one block of fluorescent overhead lights was turned on. If not for that block, the underground room would have been plunged into total blackness.

As Bryan's eyes adjusted to the darkness he saw that the menacing shadows were nothing more than piles of cardboard boxes. No doubt musty psych department archives. *There's nothing to be afraid of,* Bryan told himself as relief flooded his body so strongly, it felt almost like another wave of fear. *You know why you're here.*

A figure materialized from the shadows by the far wall of the basement. "Hello, Bryan," Dr. Akre's low, even voice intoned. "Shut the door behind you, would you please?"

Bryan obeyed, easing the door back into its frame as quietly as possible. Then he turned back to Dr. Akre. The professor had advanced a few steps, but his face was still half shrouded in shadow.

"I know what's going on," Bryan said. He fought to keep his voice as even as Dr. Akre's, despite the surge of nervous excitement he felt. "I know why I'm here."

Dr. Akre's lips curved into a smile. He laced his fingers together and cracked his knuckles. "Yes, Bryan. I know you do." He made a stifled noise that vaguely resembled a chuckle. "I've been watching you from the beginning. You learn very quickly."

Bryan beamed with pleasure. Dr. Akre's praise meant a lot to him. The man was a genius and a saint. "What do I learn next?" he asked eagerly. "I want to help you . . . any way I can."

Dr. Akre stepped back into the shadows. "I know you'll help me," he whispered. "Come with me, Bryan. I want to show you something."

Too overcome to speak, Bryan followed Dr. Akre through the darkened maze of piled-up boxes to the corner farthest from the light. To his surprise, Dr. Akre reached into the shadows and turned a doorknob that was set into a recess of the wall. *I'm sure that doorway wasn't there before,* Bryan thought, puzzled. He blinked rapidly, trying to adjust his eyes to the harsh neon glow emanating from the open doorway.

Dr. Akre paused before passing through the doorway. He turned to face Bryan, though with the bright light behind the professor's head Bryan had trouble making out his features.

"Bryan, are you ready to advance to the next level with me?" Dr. Akre asked gravely.

"Yes," Bryan breathed, scarcely trusting himself to say anything more. He knew exactly what Dr. Akre meant. Ever since the experiment had come into his life, it was as if Bryan was a whole new man. He had been reborn into a life where he saw everything much more clearly. Where he knew who he could trust . . . and who he had to watch out for. He'd never really felt alive before—not like this. And the sad thing was, he'd never even known what he was missing.

As he followed Dr. Akre into a vast, shadowy room Bryan felt himself trembling with excitement. Now that he was about to cross the threshold of Dr. Akre's secret circle, Bryan knew he was entering yet another new phase of his existence—opening up new horizons he'd never dreamed possible. He couldn't wait to find out what was waiting for him on the other side.

> Certain traits are genetically linked to gender and occur only in males due to the fact that the genetic information governing these traits is on the Y chromosome.

Nina snorted aloud at her biology textbook. "No kidding. Like the gene that controls breaking off relationships for no reason. Or maybe the gene that controls being taken in by evil scientists who want to poison your mind against your girlfriend."

It was well past midnight, and Nina was sitting at her desk, making a vain effort to take her mind off her fears and catch up on her biology reading. She was succeeding in neither.

After the terrifying incident with Kerri on the quad earlier that evening, Nina's nerves were totally rattled, and she couldn't seem to relax. There was no doubt in her mind now that her worst fears about EFC were true. Nina knew she had to get some solid evidence fast before she became the next person who knew too much and had to be "disappeared." But she'd spent hours turning the night's events over in her head and still hadn't been able to come up with any explanation of how Dr. Akre could condition a normal, intelligent woman to snap like that simply by making her watch two hours of TV a day.

Trying to deal with her homework had been a last-ditch attempt to clear her head—she'd been thinking in circles, her own mounting frustration with herself making it virtually impossible to think constructively. But as hard as she tried to concentrate on genetics, Nina kept returning to thoughts of the experiment and mentally kicking herself when those thoughts failed to lead anywhere. She was getting so tense, even random scientific facts were beginning to tick her off.

"*And* I'm talking to myself again," Nina said wryly. She bent over her book again, trying to push down all the panicked thoughts that threatened to overwhelm her.

Other genetic traits, known as X-linked traits, are situated on the X chromosome and occur with disproportionate frequency among males.

Nina highlighted the sentence absently, still wondering if it was possible that her fears were tinged with artificially induced paranoia. She kept half worrying that sooner or later she'd fall victim to the brainwashing. But when she thought

222

about it, it didn't make sense that she would be affected at a much slower rate than everyone else, any more than it made sense that she would be the only one not affected at all.

Nina reread the sentence she'd just high-lighted, realizing she hadn't really registered it the first time. "Hmmm, interesting," she commented sarcastically. Actually it *was* pretty interesting to think about the biological differences between men and women; ordinarily Nina was fascinated by science and concerned with gender issues. But right now she was just getting impatient with sitting in front of her textbook. Nina forced herself to focus on the page open before her.

> One example of an X-linked trait is red-green color blindness, which is far more common among men than among women.

In spite of her resolution to give her reading full attention, Nina rolled her eyes with annoyance. "Tell me something I don't know," she muttered, bearing down almost angrily on the sentence with her marker. Not many people knew she was red-green color blind—it just didn't come up that often—but whenever anyone found out, they reacted as if she were some kind of freakish mutation or rare specimen. And they always recited that vague statistic about color blindness being far less common among women. She'd gotten to be a little touchy about it just because she was sick of having the same conversation with people. To Nina it wasn't such a big deal that she was color blind—aside from obeying traffic lights, there weren't too many situations in which telling red and green apart mattered.

This reading is a waste of my time, Nina decided, putting the cap back on her marker. *The only biology lesson I'm interested in right now is the twisted version of science Dr. Akre's using to control people's minds.* Even if she was getting nowhere in trying to discover what was going on, it was pointless to pretend she could concentrate on anything else.

Nina tossed the marker onto her desk and covered her face with her hands, massaging her eyes and cheekbones with her palms. When she lowered her hands from her face, Nina was looking back down at her textbook. The sentence she'd just highlighted glared out at her.

One example of an X-linked trait is red-green color blindness. . . .

Red . . . green . . .

Nina furrowed her brow thoughtfully. Suddenly the words registered in a way they hadn't a moment ago. "Most people can see red and green," Nina murmured to herself, her heart

224

beginning to hammer. "Most people are really surprised when they find out I can't. So . . ."

The idea gradually formed itself in her mind, like a piece of clay spinning on a wheel. If not seeing red and green was something that made Nina different from most people—but that very few people knew about or could tell—it was just possible that her color blindness was the missing puzzle piece she'd been seeking!

The signals . . ., Nina mused. *Could they have something to do with color? With red and green?* If so, it would certainly explain how visual images could affect people so strongly—and why Nina herself had been immune.

Nina slammed her biology book shut and jumped out of her desk chair so quickly, it toppled over. *If Dr. Akre has any inkling that I'm immune to his mind control, then I'm a dead woman,* Nina thought with a shudder as she grabbed her keys from a hook by the door and raced out of her room. *I have to do whatever it takes to get that sicko locked up before he catches on to me.*

Chapter Fourteen

"Keep going," Bryan panted as he slowed to a jog. "Have to keep going." He inhaled deeply to ease the stitch in his side.

The night air was moist, the cool green grass on the quad already damp with morning dew. Bryan felt as if he were running through a fog. The humid air was too thick, choking him as it filled his lungs. He'd been running for a long time, and the pressure in his chest was intense. The corners of Bryan's vision blurred, and he was half afraid he might pass out.

But I have to keep going, Bryan reminded himself. *I have to find her.*

"Nina!" he called out desperately into the night air. But it was a cry of futility and frustration. The floodlights lining the quad illuminated nothing but empty expanses of lawn.

Bryan staggered, once again forced by his shortness of breath to slow down. He had no idea how long he'd been running around campus searching for Nina. But he was starting to get worried—*very* worried.

That night at the psych lab, Dr. Akre had told him about a fiendish plan more horrifying than Bryan had dreamed imaginable. The truth had been like a bucket of cold water hitting him in the face. When he left the lab, Bryan knew he had to find Nina before it was too late.

There had been no light under her door at Dickenson Hall, and though he'd banged on the door and screamed her name until the RA threatened to call security, she hadn't appeared. Then he'd tried her usual carrel at the library, but she hadn't been there either. So he'd just started circling the campus, racking his brain to think of where she could be.

Now he was running out of time. Every precious moment he wasted going in circles meant they were in greater danger. There was no telling what could happen if he didn't catch up with Nina. Now that he'd talked to Dr. Akre, Bryan knew just how serious a situation she was getting herself into. Poor Nina had no idea how far in over her head she was.

Bryan couldn't stand the thought of Nina running around campus all by herself, searching for information that EFC was prepared to do anything to safeguard. *Once I catch up with her, I'll be able to take care of her*, Bryan reminded himself. *I'll never forgive myself if I can't get to her in time!*

Bryan slowed to a stop, panting heavily. *If only I hadn't told Nina I was cutting her out of my life*, he cursed himself inwardly. He bent slightly and rested his hands just above his knees. *I wish I had let her know she could trust me. It's too late now—maybe she'll never trust me again.* He had to tell her that he loved her, that he wanted everything to be all right between them . . . but after all he'd said and done, Bryan wouldn't be surprised if Nina didn't believe him.

But it didn't matter—he had to try. Even if Nina hated him for the rest of her life, he had to do whatever he could to keep her out of harm's way. He wasn't thinking about himself now, just about Nina. He had to do everything he could, before it was too late. *Before Nina* . . .

He couldn't bear to think about it. Bryan lifted his head and, squinting through the tears and sweat that blurred his vision, began stumbling blindly forward again. Only one thought filled his head:

I have to find her.

"Please open, please open, please open," Nina breathed as she frantically jiggled the safety pin in the lock.

She could barely see what she was doing, but she didn't dare turn on the light. For all she knew, security guards could be patrolling the psych building. It had been easy enough to get past the work-study student on duty at the sign-in desk by saying she'd left her purse in a class-room. But she'd have no plausible excuse if she were caught trying to jimmy the lock on the door to the X212 control room.

Nina closed her eyes, trying to focus all her energy into her sense of touch. A girl on her floor at Dickenson had showed her how to do this once, when Nina had locked herself out of her room early in the year. It had seemed so easy then, but her life hadn't been hanging in the balance at the time.

If I could only keep my hands from shaking so much, I'd probably have better luck, Nina told herself, exhaling slowly to steady her nerves. When she resumed jiggling the pin in the lock, it finally turned with a tiny click, and the door swung open.

Treading softly in her canvas sneakers, Nina tip-toed into the darkened lab and closed the door behind her. Darkness engulfed her. *Is it safe to turn on a light?* she wondered, feeling along the wall with her hands. The control room was situated in the center of the floor, and she didn't think there were any windows looking out. Nobody outside would be able to tell that the light was on.

Nina's fingers found a switch, and she flipped it. A panel of neon light overhead flickered briefly, then illuminated the room with a harsh bright light.

Squinting, Nina saw that the large circular room was cluttered with carts of audiovisual equipment and stacks of tapes. In the center of the far wall, set into a recess, was an enormous TV monitor. Wires hung beneath the monitor, leading down to a separate alcove of the wall containing a complicated-looking stack of videocassette players and some other black metal control boxes Nina didn't recognize. A desk was positioned directly underneath the equipment, and its surface was covered with piles of paper and tapes.

Nina moved toward the desk and peered closely at the equipment under the TV. She could see that the wires connected to the VCRs and the other boxes led not just to the monitor above but also out through the wall behind. *Those must lead to the cubicles,* Nina realized.

She scanned the dials on each piece of equipment, trying to identify their functions. Obviously the VCR transmitted the commercials. A couple of highly sophisticated-looking pieces of machinery with digital readout screens might have been instruments that measured subjects' brain waves.

Then Nina noticed a thin black wire that led

from the back of the VCR out of the recess and down the wall. Nina turned her gaze to the surface of the desk, where the other end of the wire appeared to be buried under a stack of papers. Careful not to disturb the stack of papers, Nina gingerly moved it aside.

Underneath was a small black box. Nina bent to examine it. Two small switches on the front were marked *R* and *G*.

Red and green! Nina thought, her heart hammering in her chest. *Could it be?*

She put the stack of papers back on the box and began rifling through other piles on the desk, searching for more evidence. Under a notebook filled with thin, spidery handwriting—Dr. Akre's, probably—Nina found a videotape marked X212. Trembling, she turned on the monitor, popped the tape in the VCR, and pressed play. A stark splash screen that read For EFC Use Only appeared on-screen.

Suddenly the room came to life with the sound of screams. Nina jumped back, quickly recovering enough to turn down the volume on the monitor. She stared up at the scene playing there with curious, detached fascination.

It took Nina a while to recognize the snack bar from the unfamiliar overhead view and slightly fuzzy focus. But before long she could clearly make out a guy with a goatee, holding a woman in a white uniform captive. The bodies of students lay facedown on the ground. Nina caught sight of a familiar golden blond head. *Elizabeth!* This was obviously the security camera footage of the incident she'd described. The date and time marked in the bottom corner of the tape now resonated in her mind.

A sickening chill crept up Nina's spine. *How did this tape get here?* she wondered.

The scene changed abruptly, and flames filled a dark sky. Nina recognized the smoke-shrouded walls of Dickenson Hall. "What the . . . ," she breathed softly, her mouth hanging slightly open in bewilderment and horror. "Who could have . . ."

Then an unmistakable accented voice rang out over the background of screams and sirens. "The events taking place before you are not a series of isolated incidents," Dr. Akre's voice declared in a cool, uninflected narrator's tone. "They are the result of a revolutionary psychoscientific breakthrough known as experiment X212. My name is Dr. Charles Akre, and I am the director of this groundbreaking research project. I invite you to watch as I explain how, on a moderate budget, our small staff has produced results far in excess of even the most optimistic projections made by EFC executives at the start of this experiment."

He sounds like he's hosting Animal Kingdom,

232

Nina thought with a shudder. *A study in animal behavior—that's all those horrible incidents are to him. You'd never know people's lives were at stake.* Even as a disembodied voice-over, Dr. Akre's chilly presence was disconcerting.

The snack bar scene appeared on the TV screen once again. As the young man's ranting continued, muffled in the background, Dr. Akre's clinical voice-over went on. "As many of you know, experiment X212 was conceived as a study in the suggestibility of the human mind. For those unfamiliar with the procedure, allow me to provide a thumbnail sketch."

Nina held her breath. *This is it!* she thought. In a moment she'd have enough evidence to get Dr. Akre convicted and put an end to the horror.

"Subjects of the experiment are shown reels of advertisements selected at random. As the advertisements play, pulses of green and red light are simultaneously projected behind the film through a separate mechanism, at a level that is not consciously registered by the viewer." A computer-animated illustration demonstrated his technique. "The green and red signals have distinct psychological effects on the subjects. The green lights stimulate and intensify the subjects' cravings for the stimuli provided by the advertisements."

The screen flashed to a scene, which also

appeared to be security camera footage, of Kerri manically stuffing her face with food at the cafeteria.

"The red lights, on the other hand, intensify negative responses such as fear, anxiety, and anger. As per EFC objectives, the sessions have gradually progressed from a disproportionate percentage of green-light stimuli to an overwhelming majority of red-light stimuli." Dr. Akre's voice was thick with smugness and a hint of contempt. "And as you'll soon see, these red-light stimuli have achieved their desired effects in a much shorter time than anticipated."

To Nina's horror, a shot of Bryan yelling at her in the corridor of the psych lab appeared on the screen. *There's a hidden camera in the hallway?* Nina marveled, the hairs on her neck prickling. *That's it. I've seen enough.*

Nina stabbed angrily at the eject button several more times than was necessary. She'd found all the evidence she needed; now she had to get out before someone caught her. After what she'd just seen, Nina could hardly believe she hadn't been busted already. There were probably cameras trained on her right now.

As she shut off all the equipment she'd turned on and stuffed the videotape into the back of her navy blue corduroy pants and under her white sweatshirt, it occurred to Nina that she should have felt happy. Jubilant, even. This tape proved her worst suspicions beyond a shadow of a doubt. All she had to do was bring the tape to campus security. They'd call the police, and in a couple of hours this nightmare would be over.

But seeing herself caught on camera had filled Nina with a sickening sense of dread. As she scanned the room to make sure everything was exactly as she'd found it, worries echoed in her mind. *What else has Dr. Akre seen?* she asked herself. *And how much does he know I know?*

Bryan headed up the stairs of the psych building, feeling sick with fear and disappointment. He wasn't sure what exactly he was going to do there since he hadn't been able to find Nina. But he'd been wandering around campus for so long that he didn't know where else to go.

Should I try to find Dr. Akre? he wondered. Maybe that was the next step. But Bryan wasn't sure he could face him, considering the circumstances.

He was about to push open the door at the top of the stairs when it suddenly flew open. A young woman threw herself through the doorway and practically collided with Bryan.

"Nina?" Bryan asked, his face breaking out into a wide grin at his good luck. In a flash he understood—she'd come to the psych lab to figure out everything he already knew. The timing couldn't have been more perfect. Their terrifying ordeal was almost over—now that Bryan had found her, he didn't have to be afraid anymore. "Nina! I've been looking all over for you."

Nina gazed at him, her mouth opening and then closing. She blinked uncertainly a few times, as if she wasn't sure what to make of his excitement.

"Nina, I'm so sorry," Bryan went on in a rush. He had to get everything out all at once before he felt too guilty to continue. "I know everything now, and . . . you were right all along. I don't know how I could have done that to you. But if you can find it in your heart to trust me, please let me help you." He cradled the side of her face tenderly in his hand. "I love you, Nina. I'm so sorry I hurt you, so sorry I scared you. Could you ever forgive me? Or at least think about it?"

Nina's dark eyes sparkled with tears. "Oh, Bryan," she whispered. "Do you really mean it?"

"I really mean it." Bryan nodded solemnly.

Nina bit her lip, hesitating. Then her face melted into a warm smile. All at once she threw her arms around Bryan's neck and covered his face with kisses.

Bryan reeled at the unexpected pleasure of Nina pressing her body against him, kissing him. It had been so long since they'd been close, since he'd felt her touch. For a moment he shut his eyes and was lost in her sweet kisses. "Nina, I missed you so much," he murmured huskily.

Then he opened his eyes again and saw Nina smiling her brilliant smile at him, relief and happiness written plainly on her face. Bryan beamed at her. *Everything is going to work out fine after all,* he thought with exhilaration.

"Come on, Bryan," Nina was saying. "We have to get to the campus police before anyone finds out what we know." She slipped her arms from his neck, threaded her fingers through his, and tugged gently on his arm. "There's no time to waste."

Bryan gave her hand a reassuring squeeze as he followed her down the stairs and across the quad. He agreed with Nina—the sooner they got this over with, the better. Bryan couldn't wait until they were alone. More than anything, he wanted to grab hold of Nina and never let go.

"So I finally figured out that maybe it was because I was *color blind,* you know? And then when I got to the lab, I found out for sure about the signals being sent through red and green light, so of course that's why I wasn't affected."

Nina felt as if she'd been injected with adrenaline as she sprinted toward campus security headquarters, her hand tightly clasping Bryan's. She was practically skipping—she felt almost dizzy with happiness and relief. Now that they were both on the same side, she knew everything was going to be all right.

Bryan squeezed her hand again. "That's wonderful, Nina. *You're* wonderful."

Nina flushed with pleasure. *Bryan is himself again—he loves me again,* she whispered inwardly, almost giddy with delight at the thought. Things had changed so fast, it felt like a dream— she still couldn't believe it was true.

"So anyway, I found this tape that totally explains everything," Nina went on. She turned her eyes toward Bryan, who was gazing intently at her. Seeing his adoring face, Nina felt an unexpected pang of emotion so strong, she had to look away. "I watched enough of it to make sure it was solid evidence, and then I just grabbed it and ran out. And then I ran into you."

Suddenly Nina had the vague feeling that a piece was missing somewhere. She slowed her pace and turned back to Bryan. "Wait, you said you found out everything about the experiment, right?"

Bryan seemed to hesitate for a split second. Then he nodded. "I know about everything."

"But how—" Nina's brows knit in confusion. She slowed to a stop on the quad, tugging on Bryan's hand so that he stopped with her. "How did you figure everything out if—if you didn't get into the psych lab too? Did you—did you break in earlier tonight?"

Bryan smiled down at her. But the smile didn't reach his eyes.

"Oh, Nina," he said mockingly, squeezing her hand so tightly that she yelped in pain. But the quad was deserted—there was no one around to hear her scream, no one to hear the way Bryan's voice had suddenly gone flat. "Always asking so many questions. When are you going to learn? When, Nina?"

Nina's stomach dropped, and her blood ran cold. *He lied*, she told herself disbelievingly. *It's all a trick!* Her eyes filled with tears. It was too much to take in—a moment ago she'd been so happy, and now she felt as if her heart had been torn into pieces. Her agony over his betrayal was so great that it took a moment for its full impact to sink in.

Bryan hadn't just lied to her.

In all likelihood, he had led her to her death.

"Oh, Bryan," Nina sobbed, still clasping his hand. "Please, don't . . . I *trusted* you! How could you do this to me? How could you—"

Bryan raised his free hand over his head. As if from far away, Nina saw him bring his fist down. Then everything went black.

Chapter Fifteen

Where am I? Nina thought fuzzily as she regained consciousness.

Her eyes flickered open, but all she could see was a haze of brown shapes. Hushed voices were speaking not far away, but her muddled head couldn't make out the words.

She blinked several times, trying to clear her vision. A musty smell filled her consciousness, and Nina realized with a start that she was lying on her side on a damp cement floor. She tried to push herself up to a sitting position, but her wrists were bound behind her back.

What happened? she thought wildly, struggling to free her arms as a lump of panic rose in her throat. *What am I doing here?*

As she gradually became more aware of her surroundings Nina realized that her ankles were bound as well. Then she saw that the brown forms surrounding her were just boxes. She was lying, facing the wall, in a room with a dim greenish glow. And one of the voices speaking was obviously Dr. Akre's.

Slowly, painfully, she managed to roll herself over so that her back was to the wall. Now she could see that the room was wide and piled with dusty cardboard boxes and wooden crates—it looked like she was in a warehouse or a storage area of some kind. Judging from the mildewy smell, she was probably underground.

Nina strained to make out two figures partially blocked by a stack of boxes. After a moment she saw that one was Dr. Akre, the other Bryan. Their heads were bent close together, and they were whispering to each other, Bryan nodding furiously at everything the professor said. Something shiny and black flashed in Dr. Akre's hand as he gestured. In another second she saw that it was a gun.

Nina closed her eyes, causing the tears that had welled up to slide down her face. The sight of the gun was terrifying enough, but seeing Bryan upset her even more. The heartbreak she felt right now was worse than the throbbing lump on her head where, she assumed, he had knocked her out cold.

How could she have believed that Bryan had

gone back to his old self that easily? Maybe she'd just wanted to believe too badly—she missed him so much. Maybe it was naive, but she'd never given up hoping that Bryan would come to his senses. Now it looked like her trust in Bryan would cost her her life.

With difficulty Nina tilted up her head so that she could see a little farther into the room. Then she caught sight of something lying a few feet away under a jumbled pile of half-assembled cardboard boxes. Something that looked like . . .

A hand! Nina realized with horror. *Is someone else trapped here?* She kicked out with her bound legs, trying to maneuver herself into a better viewing position.

But before she moved more than a few inches, Nina froze. If she could have moved her hands, she would have clamped them over her mouth to keep from gagging.

Inches away from the hand was a familiar face. A lifeless face whose staring green eyes, frozen open, still held an expression of shock. Dried blood trickled from its open mouth, and what had been a warm coffee color in life was now a flat, waxy gray.

"Christian!"

"What is that wretched creature so hysterical about?" Dr. Akre frowned with annoyance, craning his head over a stack of boxes to peer at Nina. "Bryan, go see what her problem is. We can't have her making that kind of racket."

Bryan nodded obediently and headed over to where Nina was writhing on the floor, moaning and trying to wriggle free of her bonds. "He's dead—you killed him—" she gasped. With her legs pistoning out behind her, she resembled a fish on dry land, thrashing its tail.

For an instant, as he watched Nina struggle helplessly, Bryan felt a strange flash of pride mingled with pity. *Nina's really something,* he thought. *After all she's been through, she's still a fighter.*

Then he shook his head. *Where did that come from?* Nina wasn't a fighter, she was a *destroyer.* How could he have forgotten, even for a second, her evil plan to ruin Dr. Akre? Ever since the professor had explained Nina's diabolical intentions to him earlier that night, Bryan had known with total certainty that she had to be stopped. He'd eagerly agreed when Dr. Akre suggested Bryan lure Nina back to the lab by pretending to be on her side. And the way she'd fallen for it was laughable. He couldn't believe he'd felt any sympathy toward her, even for a moment.

She's even more manipulative than I thought, Bryan realized, glad that he'd managed to contain his disloyal impulses before he did something he'd regret.

He glanced at Dr. Akre, worried that the professor was intelligent enough to have somehow sensed his internal treachery. But as Dr. Akre met his eyes, Bryan saw approval on his face. His chest swelling with pride, Bryan glared down at Nina. "Keep quiet and don't move," he ordered in the hardest voice he could muster. Nina looked up at him, a stricken expression on her tear-stained face. Bryan was slightly surprised to see that her eyes were wide with fear.

"Bryan," she whispered, "please don't do this. I trust you—I know this isn't really you."

Blinking, Bryan took a step back. To his confusion, he could feel some of his confidence evaporating. What did she mean, it wasn't really him? That had to be wrong. Ever since Dr. Akre had opened up so many new frontiers to him, it was like Bryan finally *was* himself—maybe for the first time in his life. And yet . . .

In spite of himself Bryan flashed on the moment, less than an hour ago, when Nina had thrown her arms around him and covered his face with kisses. She had felt so soft in his arms, her kisses so cool on his fevered face.

The memory enveloped Bryan for a fleeting instant, filling all his senses, then slipped away like a half-remembered dream. It was as if he had once led another life, in another time and place, where he was happy. So happy . . .

No. I'm happy now, Bryan reminded himself, shaking his head.

"Bryan?" Nina whispered again, pleadingly.

Bryan jerked himself angrily back to reality. He was just allowing himself to be sucked into her web of lies and manipulations, that was all. He narrowed his eyes at Nina, fixing her with a withering stare. "Shut up!" he growled. "Just do as I say. It'll all be over soon."

Nina seemed to shrivel into the floor as Bryan glared down at her. Pain and fear were etched on her face, and for a moment Bryan's heart gave another little lurch.

"Search her," Dr. Akre barked, his voice slicing cleanly through the morass of sentimentality that was threatening to engulf him. Bryan was startled to realize that the professor had quietly come up behind him and was standing at his elbow. "Let's see for ourselves what a liar and a thief she is."

Bryan nodded. He stepped mutely forward and bent over Nina. Rolling her roughly over onto her stomach, he patted down her back, willing himself not to notice how soft and warm her body felt.

Then his hands encountered a hard, boxy shape at the small of her back. He lifted Nina's bound arms off her back, pulled up the bottom of her sweatshirt, and removed a videotape labeled X212 from where it was tucked into the waistband of her pants. He stepped back toward Dr. Akre and handed him the tape.

"Thank you, Bryan. I believe that tape belongs to me." Dr. Akre tucked his gun into the waistband of his dress slacks, opened the case, and took out the tape. As the empty case clattered to the floor Dr. Akre began yanking out foot after foot of tape. From the corner of his eye Bryan saw Nina lift her head slowly from the cement floor and turn so she could see what was happening.

"I'm afraid that you know too much about our little project, Nina," Dr. Akre continued calmly. When the tape was nothing but a jumbled knot of film stretching from his hands to the floor, Dr. Akre dropped the whole mess and crushed the plastic tape cartridge with his foot. He brushed off his hands on the jacket of his gray suit. Then he produced a book of matches from his breast pocket and lit one.

"I'm going to destroy this evidence now," Dr. Akre announced, holding the lit match up between his white fingertips. "And when I'm done, I'm going to destroy the other piece of evidence in this room—you, Nina." He lowered the match toward the floor. "As far as I'm concerned, all you are is a recording device. And I want you out of the picture."

Bryan felt an unexpected jolt of emotion as the match hit the film, turning the loops of tape into one melting, coiling mass. But it wasn't the blissful abandon he'd felt when he saw fire at Nina's dorm. This was something much more complicated—a mixture of anger and confusion, plus a hint of wistfulness he didn't understand. Bryan had seen with his own eyes—felt with his own hands, even—that Nina was out to sabotage Dr. Akre by stealing that tape. All she wanted was the evidence to undermine them. She deserved to die. *Just like Dr. Akre said.*

And yet touching her again just now, running his hands down her body . . . it made the strange, nostalgic sensation rush over him even more strongly than before. But the feeling was elusive, like the melody of an old song he couldn't quite recall.

Bryan stared at the flickering flames as they sank into the melted black mass on the floor and finally died. Only an ugly chemical odor remained. As much as Nina had hurt him, the idea of her being *destroyed* still frightened him.

But if Dr. Akre says it's necessary, it is, Bryan reminded himself. *We have to get her before she gets us.*

Nina watched the fire die out, frantically racking her brain for any excuse she could use to stall for time. She didn't know where she was, but it was possible someone had heard her scream. *I've got to keep him talking—buy some time,* she thought. It was a long shot, but she had nothing else to hope for.

As the last of the flames faded, Dr. Akre drew his gun and lifted it, aiming directly at her. "Don't worry, Nina," he said flatly. "You won't suffer. I don't care enough about you to drag this out."

"Wait!" Nina cried, shaking her shoulders back and forth in a vain effort to free her arms. "Wait, don't shoot! I wasn't trying to hurt you; I . . . I just wanted to help. I wanted . . . I thought I could take the tape to someone who would help . . . ," she stammered lamely.

Dr. Akre lowered the gun slightly. Nina saw that the corners of his mouth were turned down in a suspicious grimace. "Help?" he repeated ironically, arching one eyebrow.

"Yes, because—" Nina licked her lips nervously. She made her eyes as wide as she could. "I know there are . . . bad people . . . who are out to get you. And—I thought if we got the truth out, you would be safe."

Is he buying it? she wondered anxiously. *Do I sound brainwashed?* Nina stole a glance at Bryan and was encouraged to see that he looked bewildered, as if he didn't know what to think.

"So you wanted to help, did you?" Dr. Akre lowered the gun to his side.

"Yes," Nina practically sobbed. Now that the gun was pointing down and she was tantalizingly close to being out of danger, she felt on pins and needles, poised halfway between relief and desperate terror. "I know that—that they're all out to get us and—I don't want to let them. Please, I want to help you!" Her voice sounded hysterical in her own ears—maybe she *was* doing a good acting job. Maybe Dr. Akre would actually believe that she, like Bryan, was eager to help him.

Dr. Akre smiled a tight smile and handed the gun to Bryan. "Hang on to this while I untie our friend here, would you, Bryan?" he asked pleasantly.

Nina's heart leaped as Dr. Akre approached and crouched beside her. He leaned toward her bound wrists, then drew back and paused.

Dr. Akre looked Nina in the eyes, and a sly smile crept across his face. Then suddenly his features clouded over with anger and disgust. Before she could react, he drew his arm back and slapped her across the face.

She let out a strangled cry, cringing from the slap and shaking all over with fear. He had caught her in her lie—and now she was truly doomed.

"You fool!" the professor spat contemptuously as he got to his feet, his narrowed eyes still trained on Nina. "How stupid do you think I am? Right from the beginning I could tell from your brain scans that you weren't reacting right. You were afraid *of* me—not like the others who were afraid *because* of me. So I did a little investigating and found out about your color blindness."

Nina just gaped. Her face still stung from his slap, and her mind was reeling. *He knew all along.*

"That's right, Nina." Dr. Akre let out one of his wooden little chuckles. "I must say, I was delighted to have the unexpected luxury of a control subject. You served as a yardstick of the other subjects' progress. And you provided me with many valuable insights—the project couldn't have advanced so quickly without you. That's the only reason I let you keep running in your little circles for so long. I'd have dispatched you instantly otherwise."

Nina felt chilled to the bone. The idea of facing her death knowing she'd actually *helped* Dr. Akre advance his sick plan was more than she could bear.

"Of course," Dr. Akre went on, chuckling again, "it was highly entertaining to watch your little Batman-and-Robin routines with your unfortunate friend over there." Smirking, he inclined his head toward where Christian's dead body lay partially covered by cardboard. "So it's a shame that all this has to come to an unfortunate end. But I'm afraid that you're a bit like a lab rat: You've served your purpose for science, but it wouldn't be prudent to let you loose in the general population. Thus you'll have to be destroyed. Put to sleep, as it were."

"Please," Nina choked. "You don't have to kill me!" She glanced over at Bryan, but he was glaring at her with an expression of barely contained rage, still holding the gun at his side.

Dr. Akre chuckled dryly again. "Oh, but I'm afraid I do. That way EFC can move its mind-control project out of the experimental stage with no obstacles. Soon every member of every home in America with a TV set will be under EFC's control. So you can look on the bright side, Nina." His thin lips stretched into an impossibly wide grin. "Your loss will be science's gain."

This is it—I'm going to die! Nina's head spun wildly. She'd thought she was racing against time, that she had a chance to stop Dr. Akre before he stopped her. But all this time she'd been like a tiny fly wandering into a vast web. Every trap had already been laid in place—there was no escape.

"Why are you doing this?" Nina cried out, desperately stalling for time. At this point she had nothing to lose. "Why would EFC *want* to make everyone in America go crazy? And why would you want to help them?"

Dr. Akre shrugged, folding his arms across his chest. "I don't need to know what EFC wants. Unlike you, I don't consider it worthwhile to risk my life to get all the answers." He smirked again. "I do have a personal theory that they're hoping mass chaos will provide a convenient excuse for instituting military rule. But that's neither here nor there. What matters is that the terms of my agreement with EFC allow me to pursue science in the pure form for which it was intended."

"*Pure*? What is *that* supposed to mean?" Nina scoffed. "I never saw anything more corrupt than your twisted idea of science. You're supposed to *improve* people's lives, not ruin them!" She kept her attention focused on Dr. Akre, but from the corner of her eye she could see Bryan glancing nervously back and forth between her and the professor.

Dr. Akre glared at Nina and pressed his lips together in a pale line. "Obviously you don't see the perfect beauty of my method." For a moment his eyes took on an almost misty look. "My work explores the boundaries of the human mind and exposes just how pitifully narrow they are. The brain is nothing more than a pathetic second-rate computer processor." Dr. Akre turned his attention to Bryan and seemed to scrutinize him thoughtfully as he spoke, a mixture of pride and smugness on his hard, lined face.

"So easily dazzled by a few flashing lights," the professor mused, gazing at Bryan with as much proprietary fascination as if he had forged him out of iron. "Why do I do it, Nina? You'd never understand. No one could ever understand the thrill, the rush of programming those puny minds like robots. And of course"—he choked out his flat little laugh—"no one would ever believe how much I'm getting paid to do it." Still chuckling, Dr. Akre held his arm out to Bryan, gesturing for him to hand over the gun.

Rage and desperation coursed through Nina's body. "Bryan, don't let him treat you like that!" she shouted, struggling so fiercely that the ropes scraped skin from her wrists. "Can't you see he's brainwashed you? Listen to him! He's saying that people are robots—that *you're* a robot! Don't obey him!"

Dr. Akre dropped his arm as Bryan was about to hand him the gun and turned blazing eyes on Nina. "Shut up!" he bellowed. "Bryan wants to obey me. He is *loyal!*"

"For how long?" Nina fired back. Her heart was pounding in her throat, and she wondered wildly what she would gain by mouthing off to Dr. Akre like this. But she also knew with near certainty that if she stopped talking, he'd shoot her. "You can't just drive all these people to the breaking point and expect them to keep obeying you. Sooner or later they'll turn on you . . . and *then* what will you do?"

Dr. Akre's usually ashen face flamed an angry red. "I'll show you what I'll do," he growled, balling his hands into fists. "I'll show you just how loyal my subjects are." He turned toward Bryan. "Bryan! Since you're holding the gun, why don't *you* do the honors? Shoot her, Bryan. Go ahead . . . kill her!"

Bryan looked bewildered. He stared down at the gun in his hand as if seeing it for the first time.

Nina drew in her breath as the sharp irony of the situation stung her. Bryan—the man she loved with all her heart—was standing before her, debating whether to shoot her. The sight of him contemplating the gun was almost enough to make her lose all hope.

But I can't give up, Nina willed herself. *I have to fight for my life. I know the real Bryan is in there somewhere!*

"Bryan, don't do it!" Nina cried. "I know you don't really want to hurt me!"

She prayed silently that she was telling the truth. *Who knows how strong Dr. Akre's hold on him is?* But connecting with Bryan was her last hope. "Bryan, don't you see he's controlling your mind? You're not a murderer, Bryan. I know you're not!"

"Aim the gun, Bryan," Dr. Akre called out in a clear, even voice. "Don't listen to her—just do what you have to do."

"Bryan, no," Nina pleaded as Bryan raised the gun, staring at her with a hypnotized expression. "Remember how it used to be before all this started? Remember how much we loved each other? It's because of him that we're not together anymore! *Him!*"

"Right between her eyes," Dr. Akre ordered,

his steady voice drowning out Nina's pleas. Nina saw Bryan's hands, gripping the gun, waver in an uneven circle, then come to a stop—in a direct line with her forehead. She caught her breath.

"Bryan, I love you," she whispered. "I know you still love me. Please don't do this."

Bryan replied by cocking the gun.

Aiming the gun at the smooth expanse of forehead above Nina's soft, imploring eyes, Bryan couldn't make himself tear his gaze from hers. The idea of putting out the light of those eyes—permanently—hurt him in a way he couldn't name.

He licked his dry lips nervously. His hands were still shaking, and he squinted in an effort to focus his aim. *I've got to concentrate,* he thought. He wanted so badly to please Dr. Akre. . . .

But I don't know if I can do this, Bryan admitted to himself. Nina's eyes, her pleading voice, the way she told him she loved him—he couldn't make any of it compute with the hateful person he knew she was. *She's just trying to trick me. Right?*

But all at once Bryan wasn't sure. Confused, he lowered the gun slightly and turned to Dr. Akre. His lips parted in an unformed question.

"What are you gaping at?" Dr. Akre snapped. "Prove to me how loyal you are, Bryan. Aim the gun and *shoot her!*"

Bryan's lip quivered at Dr. Akre's harsh tone. He turned back toward Nina and raised the gun again.

"Bryan, please don't do it," Nina begged. "I know this isn't you. I fell in love with you because you were good—"

"Stop it!" Bryan screamed, blinking back tears.

"And kind, and principled—"

"Don't listen to her, you idiot!" Dr. Akre's voice hissed. "Fire! Shoot her! What are you waiting for?"

"You're not a killer, Bryan," Nina insisted. "And I know deep down you love me!"

"Do it, Bryan—now!" Dr. Akre commanded.

"Just be quiet," Bryan whispered. He felt his blood pounding in his temples. He darted a glance at Dr. Akre, lowering the gun uncertainly. "You're scaring me. . . ."

"Scaring you?" Dr. Akre's mocking voice was edged with rage. He stabbed an accusing finger at Bryan, his other hand clenched into a fist at his side. "You're pathetic, do you hear me? Pathetic!" His voice raised with every word, shrill with hysteria. "You're nothing more than a machine that I programmed! And I have no use for a piece of equipment that malfunctions. So *shoot her,* or you'll force me to destroy *both* of you!"

Bryan opened his mouth and closed it again, paralyzed by confusion and by the deafening sound of ringing in his ears. The words echoing

256

in his head—*idiot, pathetic, nothing more than a machine*—stung him like thorns.

Does Dr. Akre really think those things about me? he wondered, tears filling his eyes as the words registered. *Would he really destroy me as soon as he would Nina?*

Bryan reeled as his world swiftly turned upside down. He didn't know what or whom to believe anymore. If Dr. Akre, his hero, could call him such horrible names . . . could threaten him like that . . . if all his kind words to Bryan had just been lies . . .

Then Nina might actually be telling the truth, his mind finished unbiddingly. His head was spinning, his breath coming in ragged gasps.

"Now, Bryan! Now!" Dr. Akre cried, his words hammering through Bryan's muddled head.

Bryan pressed his eyes closed for one second of sweet relief that almost drowned out the ringing in his ears. Then he snapped them open again, and the noise rushed over him with such force that he staggered backward a couple of steps.

I don't know what to believe . . . Dr. Akre lied . . . just a machine . . . could Nina really love me?

Suddenly all Bryan wanted in the world was quiet. He didn't care about anything anymore—he just wanted to make the noise go away.

Bryan lifted the gun. His hands were steady now.

Narrowing his eyes, he aimed straight at Nina.

Every bit of her seemed to shrink—except her eyes, which grew impossibly wide—as Bryan set his sights on Nina. Something about his bearing must have betrayed the fact that he meant business this time, since the expression on her face changed from one of pleading to one of pure, abject terror. Gazing into her anguished eyes, which until a moment ago had still held a glimmer of hope and trust, Bryan realized in an instant that she had been telling the truth all along. She loved him, and he'd been horribly wrong to believe she would ever do anything to hurt him.

But it was too late. His fingers were already squeezing the trigger.

The gun went off.

Chapter Sixteen

Bang! The gunshot shattered the room; then everything was quiet. All around Nina there was only darkness.

So this is what death is like, Nina reflected, feeling strangely calm. *Funny, it's not what I expected.* Although she was now nothing more than a disembodied spirit in the darkness, alone with her own thoughts, she didn't feel as if she were floating. She wasn't looking down on her own body. In fact, she felt a lot like she was . . .

. . . lying on a cement floor, her body rigid with fear and her eyes squeezed shut.

Nina opened her eyes. *I'm alive!* she realized, her tensed muscles sagging with relief. *How did that happen?*

Craning her head around, she saw a bullet hole in the exposed wooden beam behind her.

But Bryan was aiming right at me, she thought, confused.

Nina looked up at Bryan wonderingly. To her utter astonishment, there was real warmth in his eyes as they met hers. And she could have been imagining it, but she thought she actually saw a trace of a smile on his lips.

Before she had time to fully process the look on Bryan's face, Dr. Akre let out a plaintive, in-human cry. As Nina watched helplessly from the floor, the insane professor lunged at Bryan, knocking him to the ground.

"Help!" Nina screamed at the top of her lungs. "Somebody help us!" She struggled with all her might to loosen the rope that bound her wrists and ankles while Bryan and Dr. Akre rolled around on the ground. Nina could see that Dr. Akre was gripping Bryan's wrists, but so far Bryan was holding fast to the gun.

It's no use—the rope is tied too tightly, Nina realized, giving up her futile struggle. Desperately she scanned the room for anything she could use to help free herself.

"Put the gun down, Bryan!" Dr. Akre shouted. "Do yourself a favor and give up now!"

"You don't control me anymore," Bryan growled through tightly clenched teeth. "No way are you getting away with what you did to me and Nina!"

Nina spotted a large wooden crate several feet

away and half rolled, half pushed herself toward it. Lifting herself up to a sitting position, she reached behind her and ran her hands along the crate until she found a loose board. She managed to pry the board up enough so that the nails holding it in place were exposed. Then she frantically raked her rope-bound wrists over the nails, ignoring the scratches on her forearms, until she felt the rope slip loose.

I'm free! Nina exulted, quickly leaning forward and untying her ankles.

"You'll never pin anything on me," Dr. Akre grunted. He was on top of Bryan now, pulling at Bryan's hands to pry the gun from his fingers. "I'll get off scot-free while you two drop off the face of the earth."

Nina staggered to her feet, pain shooting through her just freed legs as the blood resumed flowing through them. Every muscle in her body ached. *If I can just keep my strength up a little longer, it will all be over soon,* she promised herself, hoping it was the truth. With great effort Nina reached down and picked up the heavy wooden crate.

"You're wrong!" Bryan roared. "Nina and I aren't the kind of people you can make disappear. I want my life back—and you're going to pay for taking it away!"

Even though he was pinned underneath Dr.

Akre, his voice rang out with the strength and clarity that Nina knew and loved. Tears of joy sprang to her eyes. *Whatever else happens,* she thought, *at least I'll know that Bryan is Bryan again.*

"Dream on," Dr. Akre sneered. He brought his knee up sharply, and Bryan's body contracted in pain. Nina saw Bryan's fingers go slack, and in an instant Dr. Akre's hands were closing over the gun.

Staggering under the weight of the crate, Nina started to stumble painfully toward Dr. Akre. When she was a few feet away, she paused for breath. Then slowly, painfully, she hefted the crate over her head. Pain shot through her arms, and her legs threatened to give way under her, but she struggled to keep hold of the crate. *If I give up now, it's all over,* she reminded herself. *I've got to be strong!*

Dr. Akre began scrambling to his feet as he pulled the gun from Bryan's hands. When he was on his knees, he paused to aim the gun at Bryan.

But Nina was right behind him. Calling up all the anger, all the outrage, and all the harrowing grief that Dr. Akre's cruelty and ruthlessness had brought her, she brought down the wooden crate with every ounce of force in her body.

In an instant the crate splintered on Dr. Akre's bald head, spattering blood and shards of wood. He tipped forward with the impact, then jerked and fell backward, his head thudding against the cement floor.

Teetering over Dr. Akre on unsteady feet, Nina saw his beady eyes flutter shut. She stared down at his unconscious body for a moment.

Nina nudged the gun out of his hand with her foot and kicked it across the floor out of his reach. Then she slumped to the floor.

In an instant Bryan was beside her, his warm, strong arms cradling her. He rocked her gently in his arms as she felt her weight go completely slack.

"Nina, I'm so sorry," Bryan murmured into the crook of her neck. "I'm so glad you're all right. I understand if you never want to speak to me again, but I want you to know that I love you. I've never stopped loving you. I don't know what happened to me. Could you ever forgive me?"

Nina tilted back her head, and Bryan lifted his face in response. His eyes met hers, and Nina saw that they were full of tears.

He really means it, she marveled, her heart overflowing. She was so exhausted and spent, she couldn't think straight—she hadn't even really registered that it was all over and she was still alive—but Bryan's words filled her head. *He never stopped loving me.*

"Of course I forgive you. It wasn't your fault." Nina threw her arms around Bryan's neck and pressed herself tightly to him, burying her head in his chest. She heard him sob aloud and felt tears spring to her own eyes. "Bryan, I missed you so much."

As they clung to each other, both crying softly, time seemed to stand still. Nothing existed except the warmth and solidity of Bryan holding her in his arms.

Then she heard the door burst open. "Freeze! Police!" a voice shouted. Nina lifted her tear-streaked face toward the sound. She saw several uniformed men carrying guns swarm into the room and start to spread out.

"What's going on here?" the policeman closest to them called out. "The security guard on duty in this building reported hearing a gunshot."

"Everything's all right now," Nina said shakily, smiling gratefully up at the officer. "But that man tried to kill us." She pointed to where Dr. Akre lay unconscious on the floor.

"Are you prepared to make a statement?" the policeman said. He put his gun back into its holster and took out a small pad as two other officers bent over Dr. Akre to search him.

Nina nodded, her eyes brimming with fresh tears. She glanced over at Bryan, who smiled encouragingly at her, then took her hand and squeezed it comfortingly.

I can't believe we really made it, Nina thought in wonder as the policeman flipped open his pad and clicked a pen. She hadn't thought she would leave this room alive. And now everything had turned around as quickly as it had gone wrong in the first place. *Everything is going to be all right,* Nina repeated silently to herself, tightening her grip on Bryan's hand. *The nightmare is over.*

Chapter Seventeen

"There's the sign, up on the left. Harrington Institution, see?" Nina pointed, and Elizabeth turned the red Jeep onto the winding path that led off the highway.

"I still don't know how I let you talk me into coming here," Elizabeth grumbled as a white brick building surrounded by a barbed-wire fence came into view. "You're the one who knew her. I've changed my mind—I want to wait in the car."

"Liz, don't make me do this alone," Nina begged. "I might be the one who knows Kerri, but you were on the quad that night too. I know you need some closure on this experience as much as I do."

Elizabeth sighed. "I know, I know. I'm just not looking forward to it. What if she sees us and freaks out again?"

Paying a visit to Kerri Drohan at the mental institution where she'd been confined since the incident on the quad wasn't Elizabeth's idea of a fun afternoon. But Nina had convinced her that facing Kerri would be the best way for both of them to put the experience behind them. Even though they'd called ahead and been assured by Kerri's therapist that she was making excellent progress, Elizabeth couldn't get past a strange, deep-seated feeling of dread.

"Besides," Elizabeth added, "I don't want to miss my story. It's on in, like, fifteen minutes."

She'd done a piece for WSVU, reporting on the wave of violent incidents on campus—which, thanks to much pleading by Nina, made no mention of the experiment or EFC. Elizabeth valued her journalistic integrity more than almost anything, but Nina's chilling tale of what had happened to Christian was enough to warn Elizabeth off the idea of doing a conspiracy exposé. The piece was scheduled to air this afternoon, and even though Elizabeth had easily seen it a dozen times in the course of editing, it always gave her a little thrill to watch her stories when they were actually broadcast on air.

"So we'll watch it there," Nina said firmly. "It's not like you *won't* miss it if you stay in the car. Who knows—maybe it would even do Kerri good to watch it with us. Make her feel like she wasn't alone in all this."

"Do they even have TV sets in places like this?" Elizabeth asked doubtfully as the gates to the compound slowly opened and the guard waved them through.

"It seems like there are TV sets *everywhere*," Nina answered. "I can't get away from them, no matter how hard I try."

They drove through the well-tended grounds of the institution in silence. Finally the Jeep pulled into the lot beside the white brick building. Elizabeth took the keys out of the ignition and unlocked her door with trembling hands.

When they entered the building, Elizabeth saw a large reception desk flanked by small waiting areas containing armchairs and—as Nina had predicted—TV sets suspended from the ceiling by metal frames like the ones she'd seen in hospital rooms.

A woman with short black hair sat behind the reception desk, her fingers flying over the keyboard of her computer. As Elizabeth and Nina approached she paused in her typing and looked up from the monitor. "May I help you?" she asked in a silkily polite voice.

"We're here to see Kerri Drohan," Nina said. She pulled a yellow Post-it note from the pocket of her jeans and consulted it briefly, then looked up. "Room 432?"

The receptionist typed something into her

computer and hit return. As she scanned the monitor her brows furrowed into a frown. "I'm sorry, did you say Drohan?"

"*D-r-o-h-a-n,*" Nina confirmed. "Is anything wrong?" Elizabeth felt her sense of dread grow stronger.

The receptionist typed something else and was silent for a moment. "I'm sorry, but we don't have a patient by that name," she said finally.

"Well, could you tell us when she was discharged?" Nina asked, her voice sounding slightly higher than usual.

Pursing her lips, the receptionist punched a few more keys. Then she shook her head.

"I'm afraid I can't help you," she said. "Our records show that we have never had a patient by that name."

Nina looked as if she had been punched in the stomach. "There must be some mistake," she said hoarsely. "I called just the other day, and they told me her room number. Her therapist told me she was coming along really well." A plaintive note sounded in her voice.

"Who told you, Nina? What was the therapist's name?" Elizabeth prompted.

Nina shook her head. "I don't remember."

"Well, whoever you talked to was mistaken," the receptionist asserted. "Room 432 has been occupied by a Mr. Green for the past two years."

Elizabeth looked worriedly at Nina, whose face was ashen. She knew what her friend was wondering: Was Kerri "disappeared" too?

"Please, just check one more time," Nina urged. "Maybe she's in a different room?"

The receptionist shook her head firmly. "I've already double-checked. If your friend had ever been a patient at this facility, I would have that information here. Look, if this is some kind of joke—"

"No, I . . ." Nina opened her mouth to protest, but the words seemed to die in her throat.

"We must have been misinformed," Elizabeth supplied, darting a just-let-it-go look at Nina. "Maybe we can come back another time if we figure out what we got wrong."

"I guess," Nina mumbled in agreement, turning reluctantly away from the counter with a deeply troubled look on her face.

"So much for closure," Nina said dryly when they were out of earshot of the receptionist.

"Look," Elizabeth began in a low voice, "we can try checking the student directory and see if maybe Kerri used another na—"

"It's no use, Liz," Nina cut in. "Don't you see what's happened? Kerri's gone. Disappeared. They—whoever *they* are—must have thought that if she recovered enough to be a credible witness, she'd pose a threat."

"But that's impossible," Elizabeth argued,

shaking her head determinedly so her golden blond ponytail whipped around her face. "How would they find her? How would they know—"

"I don't know," Nina answered grimly. "But I know it doesn't pay to underestimate them."

She fell silent, and Elizabeth pondered the situation. Nina had a point—the conspiracy *did* seem farther-reaching than either one of them would have dreamed. But the idea that EFC had somehow tracked down Kerri and erased her out of existence . . .

It just doesn't seem possible, Elizabeth decided critically. *I'll wait until Nina's less shaken up and try bringing it up again. Maybe if we have a little more perspective on this whole experience, we'll figure out what really happened to Kerri.*

They had reached the front door when Elizabeth snapped her fingers, realizing that in her preoccupation she'd forgotten something. "My story!" she exclaimed. "Nina, do you mind if we go back for just a second?"

Nina looked as anxious to get out of the Harrington Institution as Elizabeth had been reluctant to enter it, but she nodded and, in step with Elizabeth, turned around the way they'd come.

"Excuse me," Elizabeth said to the receptionist when they'd reached the other side of the room. "Sorry to bother you again, but would you mind if I turned one of your TVs to WSVU for a minute?"

271

The receptionist looked up from her typing and gave a curt, dismissive nod that indicated she didn't care what they did as long as they left her alone. Elizabeth murmured her thanks and headed over to the waiting area.

"Rats, we missed the first five minutes," Elizabeth muttered, glancing at her watch. She quickly clicked the remote to WSVU.

A shrill, steady note filled the air as the screen was covered with bright vertical bands of color. "What the . . . ," Elizabeth breathed.

Nina came up behind her and stood at her shoulder. "I think this is some of your finest work," she remarked dryly.

"I don't understand," Elizabeth said hoarsely. "How could they make a mistake like this at the station? I cued up the tape myself two hours ago!"

She changed the channel, then turned back to WSVU, as if by doing so she might make something different appear. But the test pattern glared back at her, its noxious noise ringing in her ears. "Some intern is going to be in big trouble," she declared.

The receptionist craned her head over the desk, looking annoyed. "Would you two mind turning that down?" she asked sharply.

"Sorry," Elizabeth mumbled, shutting off the TV. "We were just leaving."

"Maybe it wasn't a mistake," Nina suggested

272

as they headed once more toward the exit. "And maybe it wasn't the crew at the station."

"What do you mean?" Elizabeth asked, frowning.

"I mean," Nina answered, sounding weary, "maybe your story was 'disappeared,' just like . . . just like Kerri. Isn't it kind of a coincidence that the one story WSVU totally fails to air would be the one about the attacks?"

As they passed through the front door Elizabeth opened her mouth to protest, then closed it again as Nina's words sank in. It all seemed so unlikely. *But so did all of Nina's other theories about EFC,* Elizabeth admitted silently. *And those turned out to be right.* Besides, it was undeniably suspicious for WSVU to just broadcast dead air like that. In all the time she'd been with the station, there'd never been such a major on-air glitch.

Dead air. It suddenly seemed like a sinister expression. In spite of the afternoon sunlight that shimmered off the black concrete of the parking lot, Elizabeth shivered.

"Well, Nina, this is one time when I *don't* think I want to know the truth," Elizabeth resolved as she unlocked the driver's side of the Jeep. "Because if you're right . . . then whoever took my piece off the air was doing me a favor." As she got in and stretched across the interior to unlock the passenger-side door, she gave Nina a tight smile. "After all, it's better that the story disappear than I do."

Nina nodded as she slid into the Jeep. "I completely agree, Liz. Just try to put the whole thing behind you. I only wish I could do the same."

"Hey, give that back!" Nina shrieked at the top of her lungs. "I need that—you can't just take it from me, you dirty thief!"

"Oh yeah? Try and make me." Laughing, Bryan held the biology book over his head, out of Nina's grasp. He didn't mind one bit that she was climbing all over him in an effort to snatch her textbook back. They'd supposedly gotten together to study. But sitting beside Nina on her bed and actually trying to concentrate on his schoolwork had been pure torture—he'd been aching so strongly to touch her that he'd resorted to playing a juvenile game of keep away.

Bryan hadn't cracked a book in weeks, and he had mountains of reading to catch up on. But right now there was no way he could focus on his work. He was aware of nothing except Nina's presence, drawing his attention like a magnet. In faded jeans and a white V-neck T-shirt that contrasted exquisitely with her dark skin, she was a radiant vision. *I still can't believe she took me back,* he marveled. *Nina must be the most amazing woman in the world. I don't know what I would do if I lost her.*

"I'm not kidding—I have a quiz next week." Nina poked Bryan in the exact spot on his rib cage where he was most ticklish. Reflexively Bryan's side scrunched up, and he let go of the textbook. It bounced onto the bed. "Ha!" Nina cried triumphantly, lunging for her book.

Bryan caught her up in his arms and rolled her over, pinning her down on the bed. "Not so fast, baby," he murmured in an exaggeratedly throaty parody of a Casanova voice. "I've got the only biology lesson you'll ever need right here."

Nina burst into giggles and kicked the bed with her feet, pretending to struggle. "Help me! I've been kidnapped by a giant cheeseball!"

Bryan grinned down at her. He was about to make another joke, but as he gazed raptly at Nina's face, he suddenly found that he couldn't speak.

The grin on his face softened into a tender smile. With laughter sparkling in her eyes, with her dark hair fanning out in soft waves around her head, Nina was indescribably beautiful. Holding her close like this, Bryan couldn't imagine anywhere he'd rather be, anyone he'd rather be with. The thought of how close he'd come to letting her slip away filled him with a bittersweet rush of emotion.

Bryan reached down and tucked a stray lock of Nina's hair behind her ear. Mesmerized by her face, he ran his fingertip down her cheek, then gently traced the line of her mouth. Then he bent his face close to hers and planted a soft, almost reverent kiss on her lips.

"I'm sorry. I know you have work to do," he whispered at last. "But you can't blame me for wanting to make up for lost time. I feel like I'm waking up from a bad dream, Nina—I can't believe after all the horrible stuff I did, you're still being so sweet to me." His voice broke slightly. "I don't know how I can ever make it up to you, but I'm going to try. I'll do whatever you want— all you have to do is say the word."

Nina's eyes shone with tears of happiness. "Just being Bryan again is more than enough," she assured him softly. A coy smile stole across her face. "But a kiss would be nice too."

Bryan leaned in and kissed Nina with all the passion and urgency that the idea of losing her had built up inside him. He ran his fingers through her hair, then down the sides of her arms. He wanted to memorize everything about Nina—the shape of her body, the smoothness of her skin, the smell of her hair—so he could never forget again, even for an instant, how wonderful it felt to be near her.

Abruptly the shrill jangle of the ringing phone intruded upon the romantic mood.

After a second Nina broke away from Bryan's kiss. Bryan opened his mouth to tell her to let the machine pick up, but she put her finger over his lips to silence him. "It might be important," she said breathlessly.

Bryan pretended to pout as he turned onto his side. Nina rolled her eyes, but a grin twitched at the corners of her mouth. She got up from the bed and went to her desk to answer the phone.

"Hello?" Nina asked. "Yes, this is Nina Harper. Who's this, please? Oh, hello, Officer! What can I do for you?"

Bryan sat up straight. He stared intently at Nina as she gripped the receiver wordlessly. It had been almost a week since Dr. Akre had been arrested and they'd made their statements, and until now there hadn't been any kind of follow-up from the police.

"Uh-huh . . . well, that's great news, right? Oh . . ." Her mouth hung slightly open, as if she'd been cut off by the person on the other end of the line.

As Nina listened, her mouth closed and set into a grim line. Bryan watched with concern as a stricken look passed over her face. *What could have gone wrong?* he wondered. *Dr. Akre was so arrogant, he got sloppy. There should have been more than enough evidence to convict him.* The cops had told Bryan that DNA tests on Christian's body would almost definitely identify Dr. Akre if he was indeed the killer.

"You're kidding!" Nina gasped. "Are they sure?" Another long pause. "I see. . . . Well, I guess there's nothing more we can do, then." Her voice quavered. "Thanks for calling. You too. Good night."

"What happened, Nina? What's wrong?" Bryan asked as she hung up the phone.

Nina went to sit back down on the bed, feeling dazed. Bryan moved close to her and put a comforting arm around her shoulders.

She took a deep breath. "That was the arresting officer calling to say that Dr. Akre is being charged with first-degree murder. They found some of his skin cells under Christian's fingernails." She shuddered, and Bryan squeezed her closer to him. "And he's also being charged with two counts of attempted murder."

"So what's the catch?" Bryan ventured. "You didn't sound like you were getting good news."

Nina slipped her arm around Bryan's waist and leaned her head against his chest. "Dr. Akre may be charged with murder, but the charges of conspiracy we filed have also been dropped . . . for lack of evidence. Bryan, they looked in the psych lab and found nothing. No equipment. No tapes. No trace of experiment X212."

"So Dr. Akre got somebody to move the equipment?" Bryan asked, sounding as if he wasn't quite sure what she was getting at.

Nina lifted her head and looked up at Bryan. *He has no idea how far this goes,* she realized. *His mind was too fried for him to realize what was going on.*

"Bryan, it's more than just the equipment." She took his free hand in hers and gave it a squeeze. "Nowhere at SVU is there *any* record of the experiment. There's no evidence that SVU has ever received funding from EFC, directly or indirectly. And the psych department says that they're having trouble locating any papers relating to Dr. Akre's membership in the faculty."

Bryan looked perplexed. "So . . . this is all a big cover-up?"

Nina nodded. "I think it's part of the conspiracy. I don't know how, but EFC seems to have ways of making the evidence against them disappear. This is serious stuff, Bryan—the officer also told me that he checked into the case files of the violent incidents connected to the experiment, and somehow they've all been made confidential. All the charges against the students who committed those violent crimes have been dropped. The police can't even track down their names—they don't seem to have ever been on file."

"I never even knew any of the other students' names besides Kerri's," Bryan mused.

"Well, she's vanished too," Nina informed him. She recounted her and Elizabeth's attempt to visit Kerri the previous day and how Elizabeth's WSVU broadcast hadn't aired. "It's like there's no limit to what they can control," she concluded. "We can't even get in touch with the other subjects because they've carefully erased all the records."

"They probably don't even realize what they were involved in," Bryan pointed out. "I sure don't."

"So while their test subjects are oblivious, EFC is free to move its brainwashing plan into the next phase, whatever that might be," Nina concluded. "This nightmare may be over for us, but who knows what EFC is still planning . . . for everyone?"

Bryan shook his head slowly as he tried to absorb everything Nina had just told him. He knew he'd been used as a guinea pig, but he'd been too focused on putting his life back together to think much about what he'd been a guinea pig *for*.

"The important part is that it *is* over for us," Bryan said finally, snapping back to the present. He squeezed Nina's shoulder. "EFC obviously severed their ties to Dr. Akre pretty neatly, so this incident is all wrapped up as far as they're concerned."

Bryan spoke decisively, hoping to convince himself as well as Nina. "They're probably doing us a favor by making sure it goes on record as a simple murder case. If we went ahead with those conspiracy charges, we could be putting our own lives in danger."

"I guess," Nina said hollowly.

"Trust me, Nina. We can relax now. We're safe." Bryan looked down at Nina, trying to meet her eyes, but she was staring off into space with a troubled, thoughtful expression. "Dr. Akre will be locked up for a long time."

"I hope so," Nina said softly. "I hope you're right about everything."

Bryan cupped her chin in his hand and tilted her face up to meet his. "I know I'm right. We're going to go on with our lives, and you know what else? I promise you that if nothing else, one very important thing has come out of this experience." He gazed earnestly at Nina, his heart swelling with love. "I am never, ever going to take you for granted again."

"I'm going to hold you to that, you know." Nina smiled as she settled back into Bryan's arms, snuggling her face against his clean-smelling cotton T-shirt. She closed her eyes and was still for a moment, feeling the rise and fall of his chest against her cheek. In Bryan's warm, comforting embrace, it was easy to believe that everything was going to be fine. The idea of the conspiracy seemed vague and far away. Unless she stopped to think about it . . .

Nina opened her eyes. "But isn't it just a little

unsettling that EFC is getting away with all this?" she asked worriedly. "Shouldn't we try to do something?"

Bryan sighed wearily and began to stroke her hair. "Nina, things don't always get wrapped up neatly like they do on TV."

Nina groaned and lifted her head to look at Bryan. "I guess you're right. But do me a favor—*don't* mention TV again for a while."

"No argument here." Bryan lowered his face toward hers. "In fact, if you want, we don't have to talk at all."

As Bryan kissed her Nina felt the last of her anxiety slipping away. *He's right—we're alive, we're safe, and we're together. That's what matters.* In a strange way the experiment had served its purpose—after going through that harrowing experience together, Bryan and Nina were closer than ever. This was nothing if not a new beginning for their relationship.

"So," Nina breathed when they pulled apart for air, "since we're obviously not going to get any work done, how should we spend the evening?"

"I feel fine about *this* activity," Bryan declared, squeezing Nina tighter in his arms.

"You just don't want to take me anywhere, you cheapskate," Nina scoffed playfully.

"Not exactly," Bryan murmured as he leaned in to kiss her. "I just want to hold you and not let go. Because from now on, I'm never going to let you forget that every second I spend with you is precious to me."

Their lips met, and Nina felt as if a current of electricity were running through her whole body. *What ever made us think there was anything wrong with our relationship?* she wondered giddily, wrapping her arms around Bryan's neck as they kissed passionately. *Everything seems just perfect to me.*

SWEET VALLEY HIGH™

Created by Francine Pascal

The top-selling teenage series starring identical twins Jessica and Elizabeth Wakefield and all the friends at Sweet Valley High. Don't miss the lastest mini-series published as part of this successful series!

ROMANCE TRILOGY
101. THE BOYFRIEND WAR
102. ALMOST MARRIED
103. OPERATION LOVE MATCH
Now available as one three-in-one collection!

HORROR IN LONDON MINI-SERIES
104. LOVE AND DEATH IN LONDON
105. A DATE WITH A WEREWOLF
106. BEWARE THE WOLFMAN

LOVE AND LIES MINI-SERIES
107. JESSICA'S SECRET LOVE
108. LEFT AT THE ALTAR!
109. DOUBLECROSSED
110. DEATH THREAT
111. A DEADLY CHRISTMAS

WINNERS AND LOSERS MINI-SERIES
112. JESSICA QUITS THE SQUAD
113. THE POM-POM WARS
114. 'V' FOR VICTORY
Now available as one three-in-one collection!

DESERT ADVENTURE MINI-SERIES
115. THE TREASURE OF DEATH VALLEY
116. NIGHTMARE IN DEATH VALLEY
Now available as one two-in-one collection!.

LOVING AMBITIONS MINI-SERIES
117. JESSICA THE GENIUS
118. COLLEGE WEEKEND
119. JESSICA'S OLDER GUY

RIVALRIES MINI-SERIES
120. IN LOVE WITH THE ENEMY
121. THE HIGH-SCHOOL WAR
122. A KISS BEFORE DYING

CAMP ECHO MINI-SERIES
123. ELIZABETH'S RIVAL
124. MEET ME AT MIDNIGHT
125. CAMP KILLER

DARK SHADOWS MINI-SERIES
126. TALL, DARK, AND DEADLY
127. DANCE OF DEATH
128. KISS OF A KILLER
129. COVER GIRLS
130. MODEL FLIRT

FLAIR MINI-SERIES
129. COVER GIRLS
130. MODEL FLIRT
131. FASHION VICTIM

CHATEAU D'AMOUR MINI-SERIES
132. ONCE UPON A TIME
133. TO CATCH A THIEF
134. HAPPILY EVER AFTER

FIRESTORM MINI-SERIES
135. LILA'S NEW FLAME
136. TOO HOT TO HANDLE
137. FIGHT FIRE WITH FIRE